SUPER POTATO
#10 SUPER POTATO'S MIDDLE AGES ADVENTURE

ARTUR LAPERLA

Graphic Universe™ • Minneapolis

Story and illustrations by Artur Laperla
Translated from the Spanish text by Norwyn MacTíre

First American edition published in 2023 by Graphic Universe™

Graphic Universe™
An imprint of Lerner Publishing Group, Inc.
241 First Avenue North
Minneapolis, MN 55401 USA

For reading levels and more information, look up this title at www.lernerbooks.com.

Main body text set in CCWildWords. Typeface provided by Comicraft.

Library of Congress Cataloging-in-Publication Data

Names: Laperla (Artist), author, illustrator. | MacTire, Norwyn, translator.
Title: Super Potato's middle ages adventure / Artur Laperla ; translation by Norwyn MacTíre.
Other titles: Super Patata (Series). English
Description: First American edition. | Minneapolis : Graphic Universe, 2023. | Series: Super Potato ; book 10 | Audience: Ages 7–11 | Audience: Grades 2–3 | Summary: Super Potato is on a time-travel mission, searching the Middle Ages for a scientist trapped in the past, and he soon finds a heroic knight who turned into a serpent.
Identifiers: LCCN 2022013320 (print) | LCCN 2022013321 (ebook) | ISBN 9781728459530 (library binding) | ISBN 9781728478302 (paperback) | ISBN 9781728480848 (ebook)
Subjects: CYAC: Graphic novels. | Superheroes—Fiction. | Potatoes—Fiction. | Time travel—Fiction. | Middle ages—Fiction. | Humorous stories. | LCGFT: Humorous comics.
Classification: LCC PZ7.7.L367 Sup 2023 (print) | LCC PZ7.7.L367 (ebook) | DDC 741.5/973—dc23/eng/20220428

LC record available at https://lccn.loc.gov/2022013320
LC ebook record available at https://lccn.loc.gov/2022013321

Manufactured in the United States of America
1-51269-50289-7/11/2022

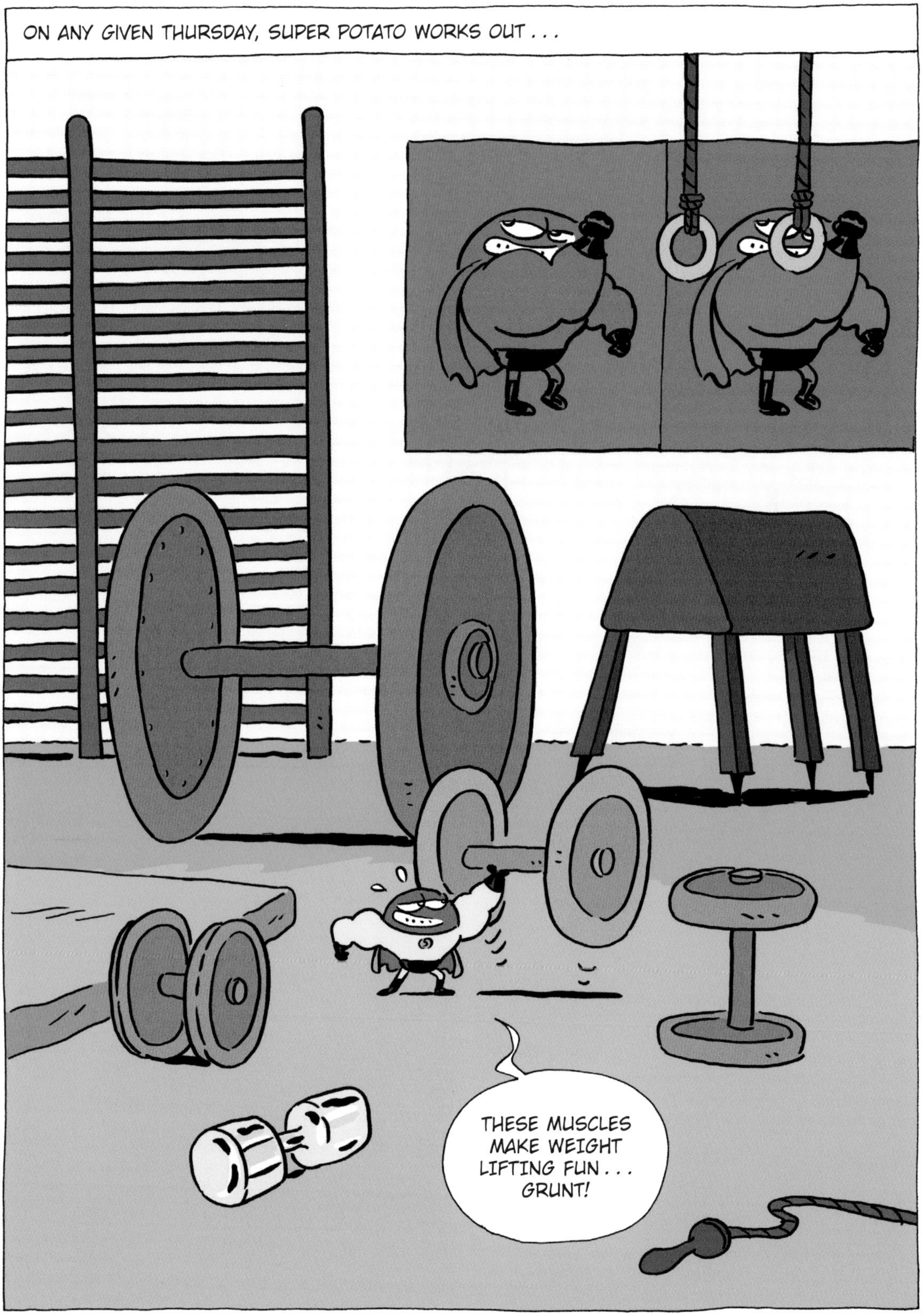
ON ANY GIVEN THURSDAY, SUPER POTATO WORKS OUT . . .
THESE MUSCLES MAKE WEIGHT LIFTING FUN . . . GRUNT!

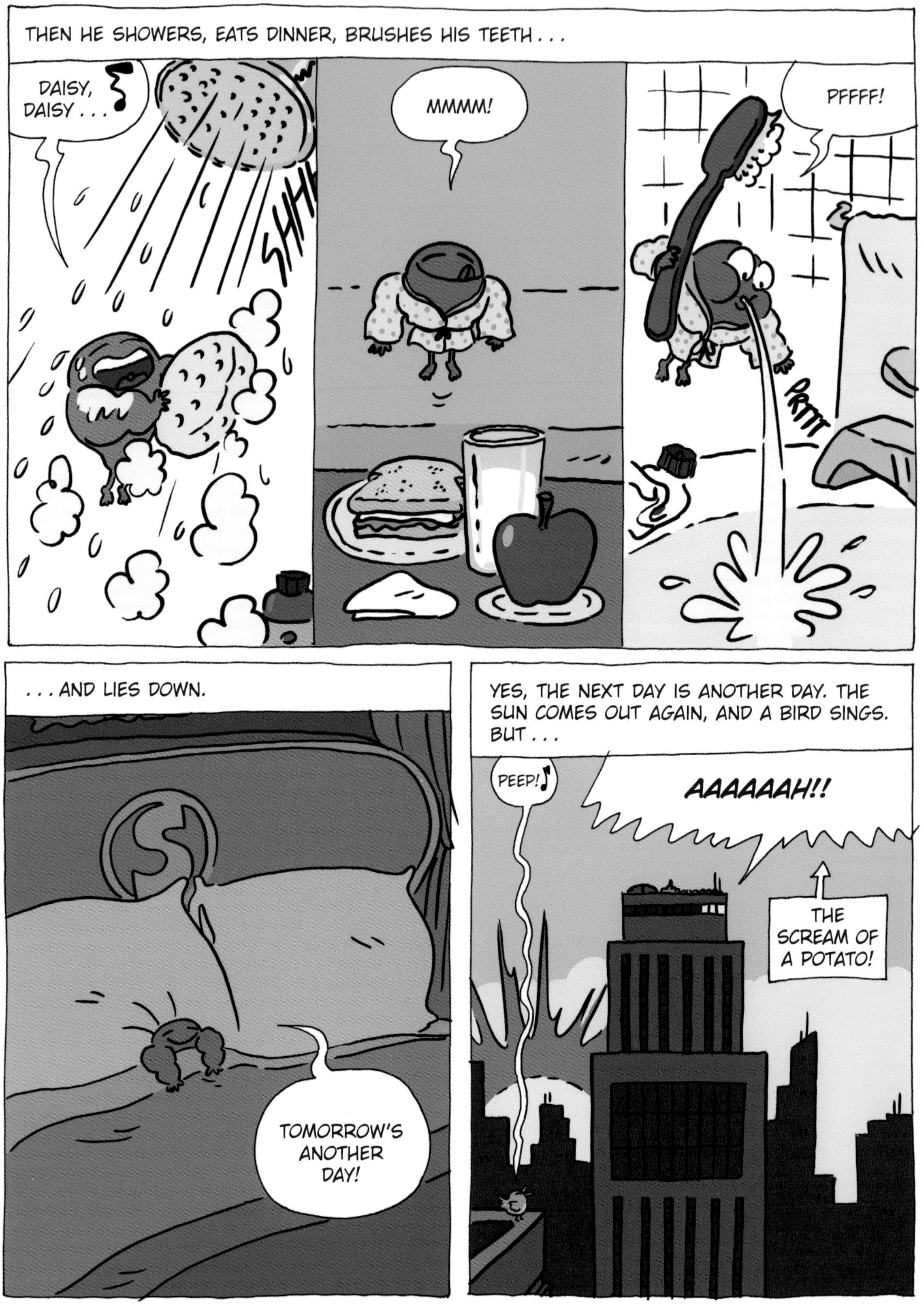
THEN HE SHOWERS, EATS DINNER, BRUSHES HIS TEETH . . .
DAISY, DAISY . . .
SHH
MMMM!
PFFFF!
PRTTT
. . . AND LIES DOWN.
TOMORROW'S ANOTHER DAY!
YES, THE NEXT DAY IS ANOTHER DAY. THE SUN COMES OUT AGAIN, AND A BIRD SINGS. BUT . . .
PEEP!
AAAAAAH!!
THE SCREAM OF A POTATO!

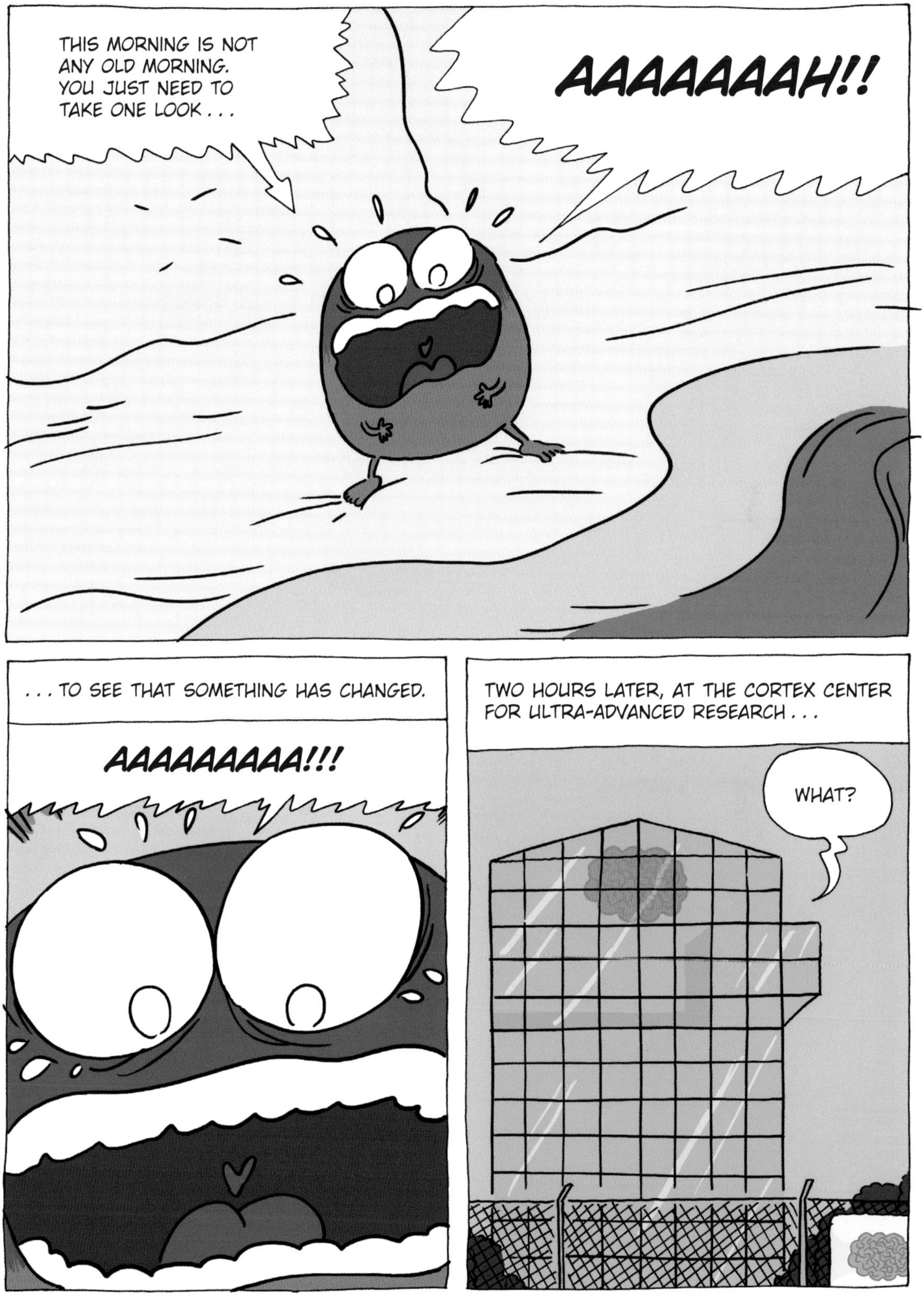
THIS MORNING IS NOT ANY OLD MORNING. YOU JUST NEED TO TAKE ONE LOOK . . .
AAAAAAAH!!
. . . TO SEE THAT SOMETHING HAS CHANGED.
AAAAAAAAA!!!
TWO HOURS LATER, AT THE CORTEX CENTER FOR ULTRA-ADVANCED RESEARCH . . .
WHAT?

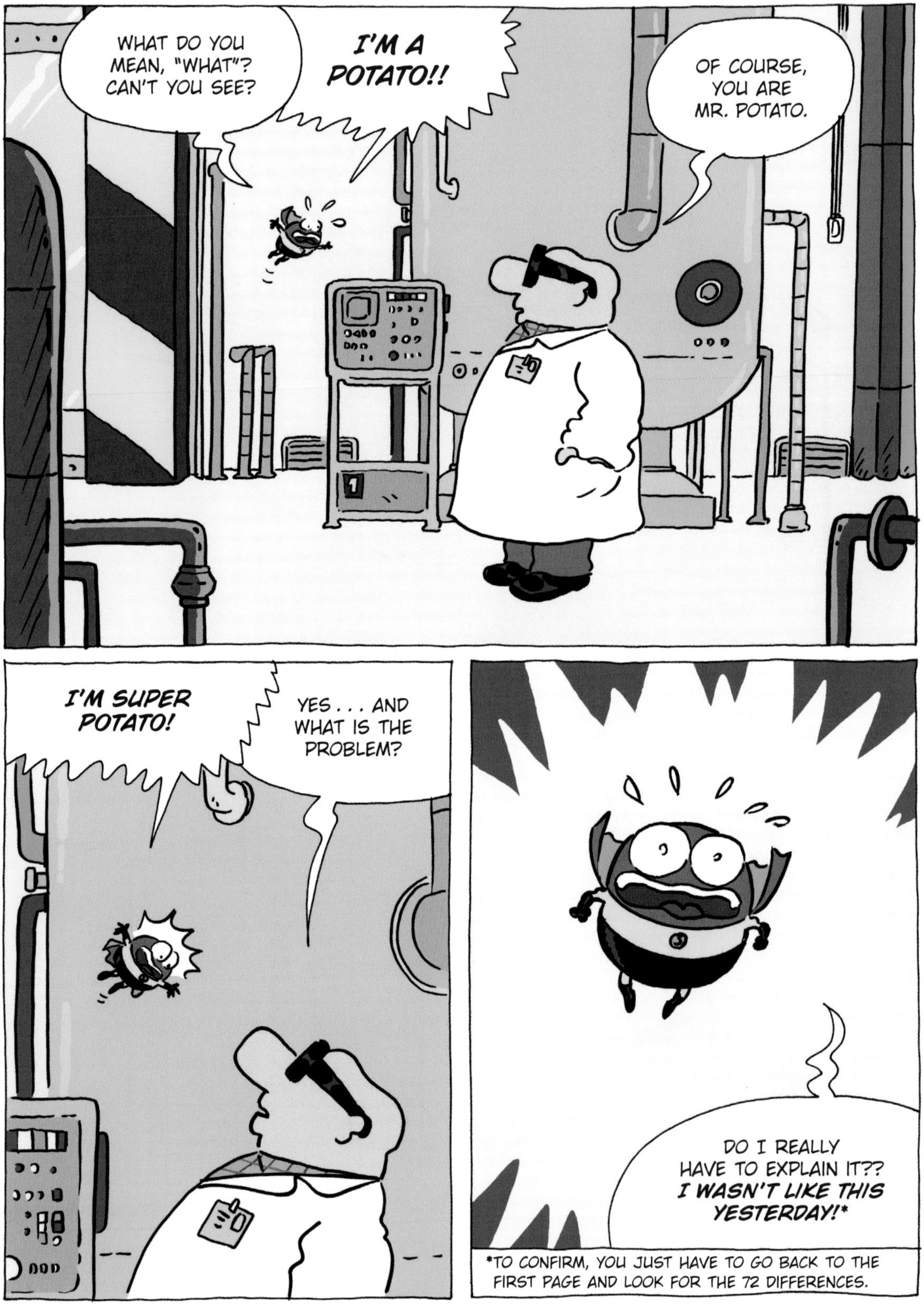
WHAT DO YOU MEAN, "WHAT"? CAN'T YOU SEE?
I'M A POTATO!!
OF COURSE, YOU ARE MR. POTATO.
I'M SUPER POTATO!
YES . . . AND WHAT IS THE PROBLEM?
DO I REALLY HAVE TO EXPLAIN IT?? I WASN'T LIKE THIS YESTERDAY!*
*TO CONFIRM, YOU JUST HAVE TO GO BACK TO THE FIRST PAGE AND LOOK FOR THE 72 DIFFERENCES.

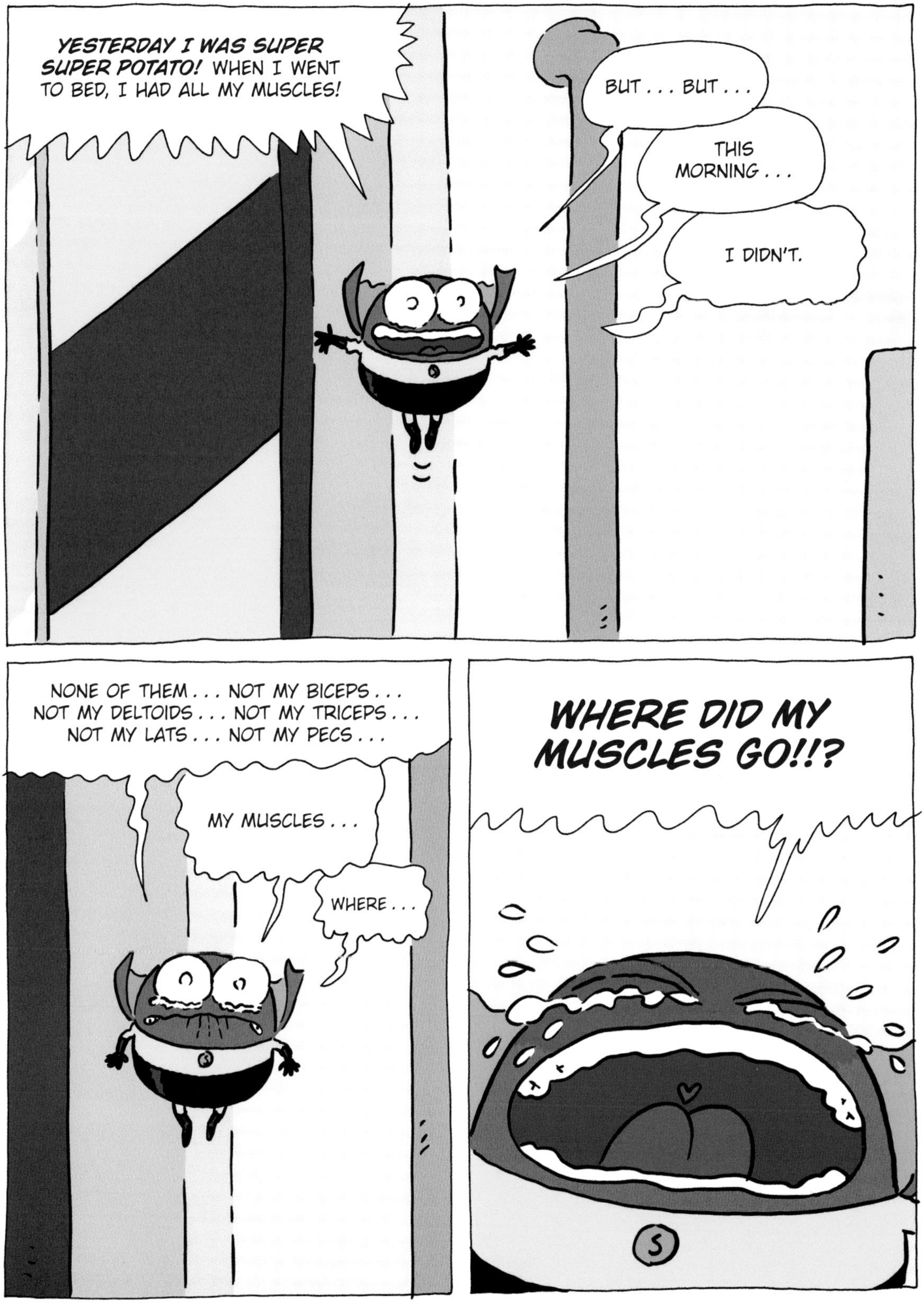

YESTERDAY I WAS SUPER SUPER POTATO! WHEN I WENT TO BED, I HAD ALL MY MUSCLES!
BUT . . . BUT . . .
THIS MORNING . . .
I DIDN'T.
NONE OF THEM . . . NOT MY BICEPS . . . NOT MY DELTOIDS . . . NOT MY TRICEPS . . . NOT MY LATS . . . NOT MY PECS . . .
MY MUSCLES . . .
WHERE . . .
WHERE DID MY MUSCLES GO!!?

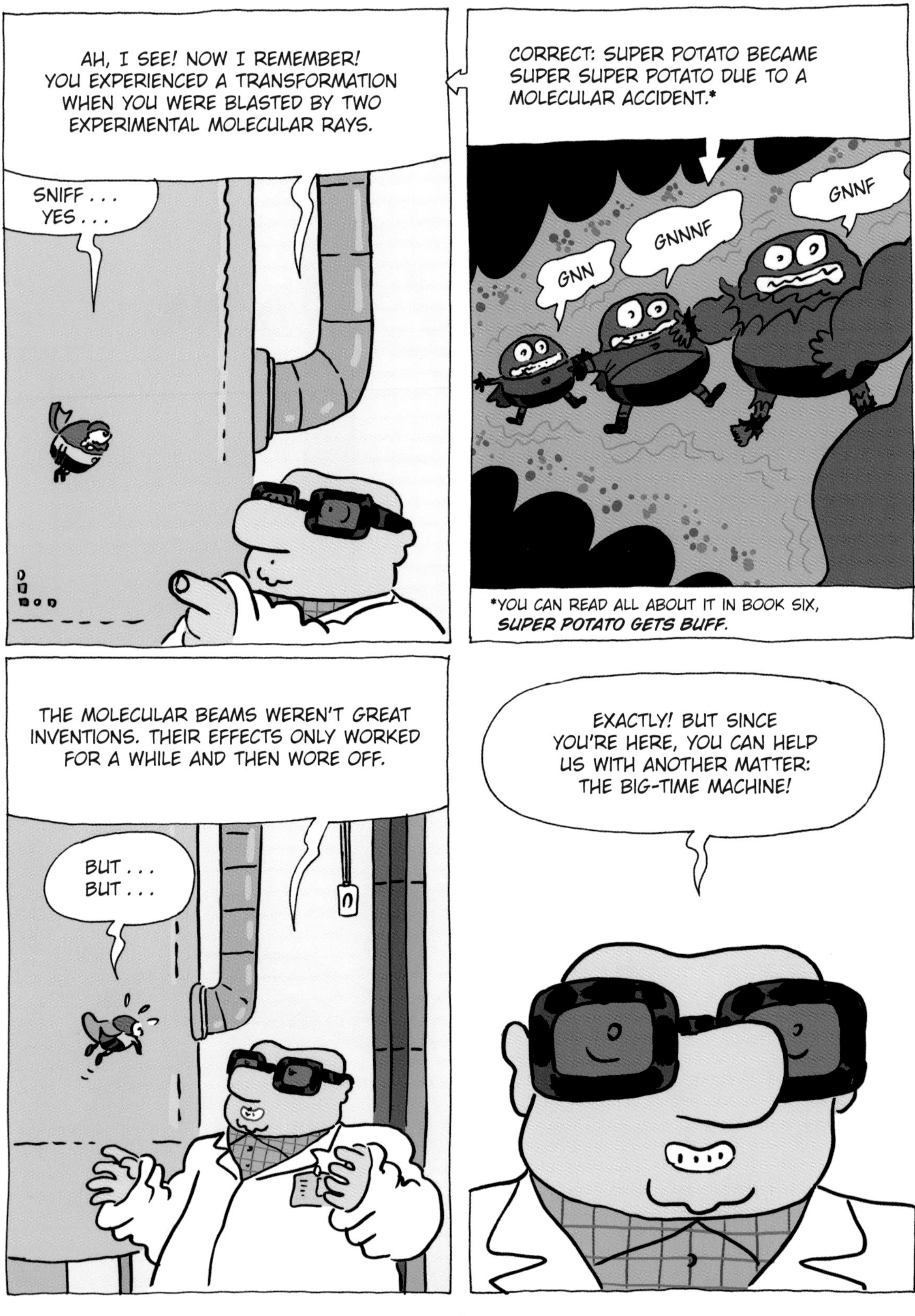
AH, I SEE! NOW I REMEMBER! YOU EXPERIENCED A TRANSFORMATION WHEN YOU WERE BLASTED BY TWO EXPERIMENTAL MOLECULAR RAYS.
SNIFF . . . YES . . .
CORRECT: SUPER POTATO BECAME SUPER SUPER POTATO DUE TO A MOLECULAR ACCIDENT.*
GNN
GNNNF
GNNF
*YOU CAN READ ALL ABOUT IT IN BOOK SIX, SUPER POTATO GETS BUFF.
THE MOLECULAR BEAMS WEREN'T GREAT INVENTIONS. THEIR EFFECTS ONLY WORKED FOR A WHILE AND THEN WORE OFF.
BUT . . . BUT . . .
EXACTLY! BUT SINCE YOU'RE HERE, YOU CAN HELP US WITH ANOTHER MATTER: THE BIG-TIME MACHINE!

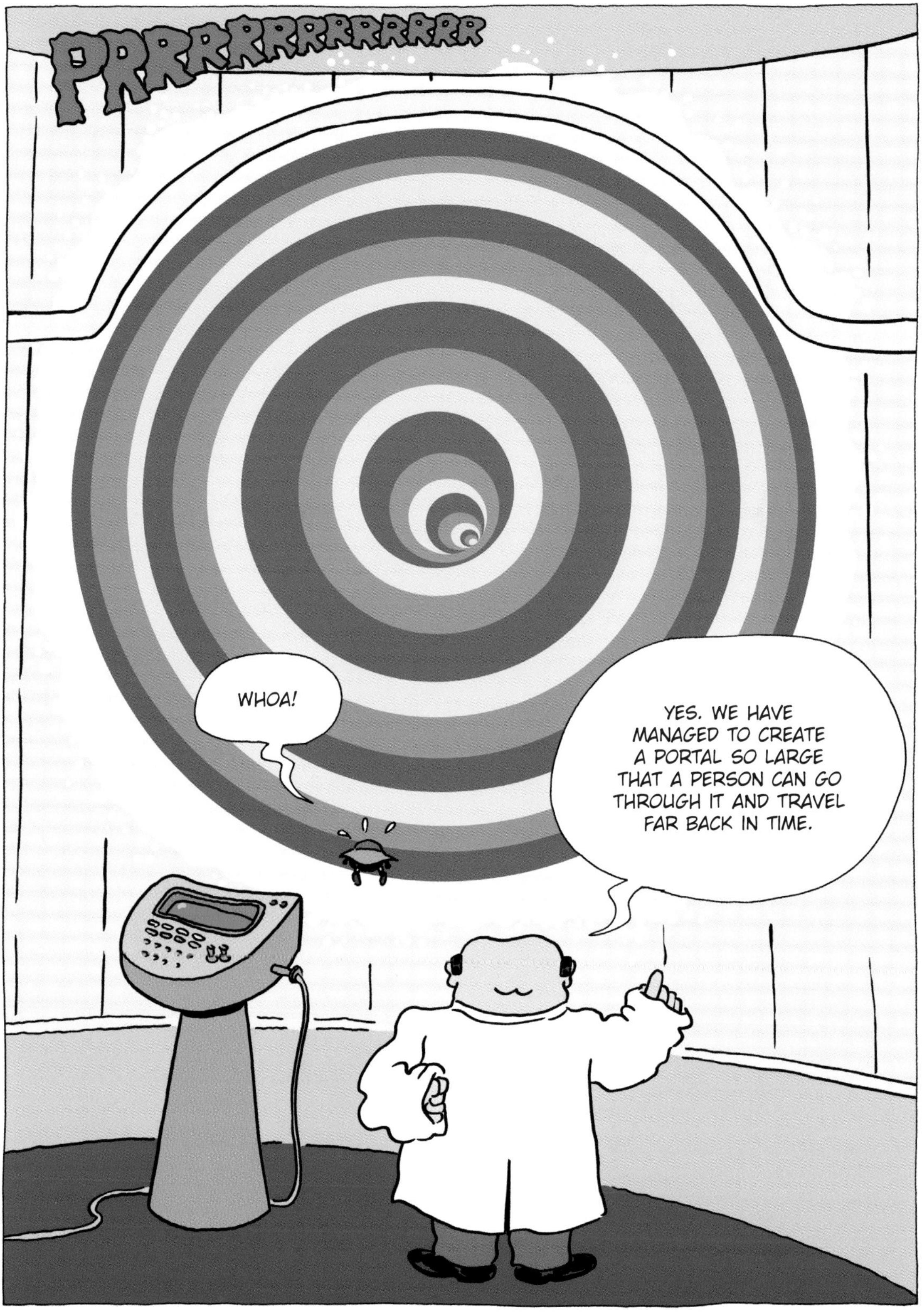
PRRRRRRRRRRRR
WHOA!
YES. WE HAVE MANAGED TO CREATE A PORTAL SO LARGE THAT A PERSON CAN GO THROUGH IT AND TRAVEL FAR BACK IN TIME.

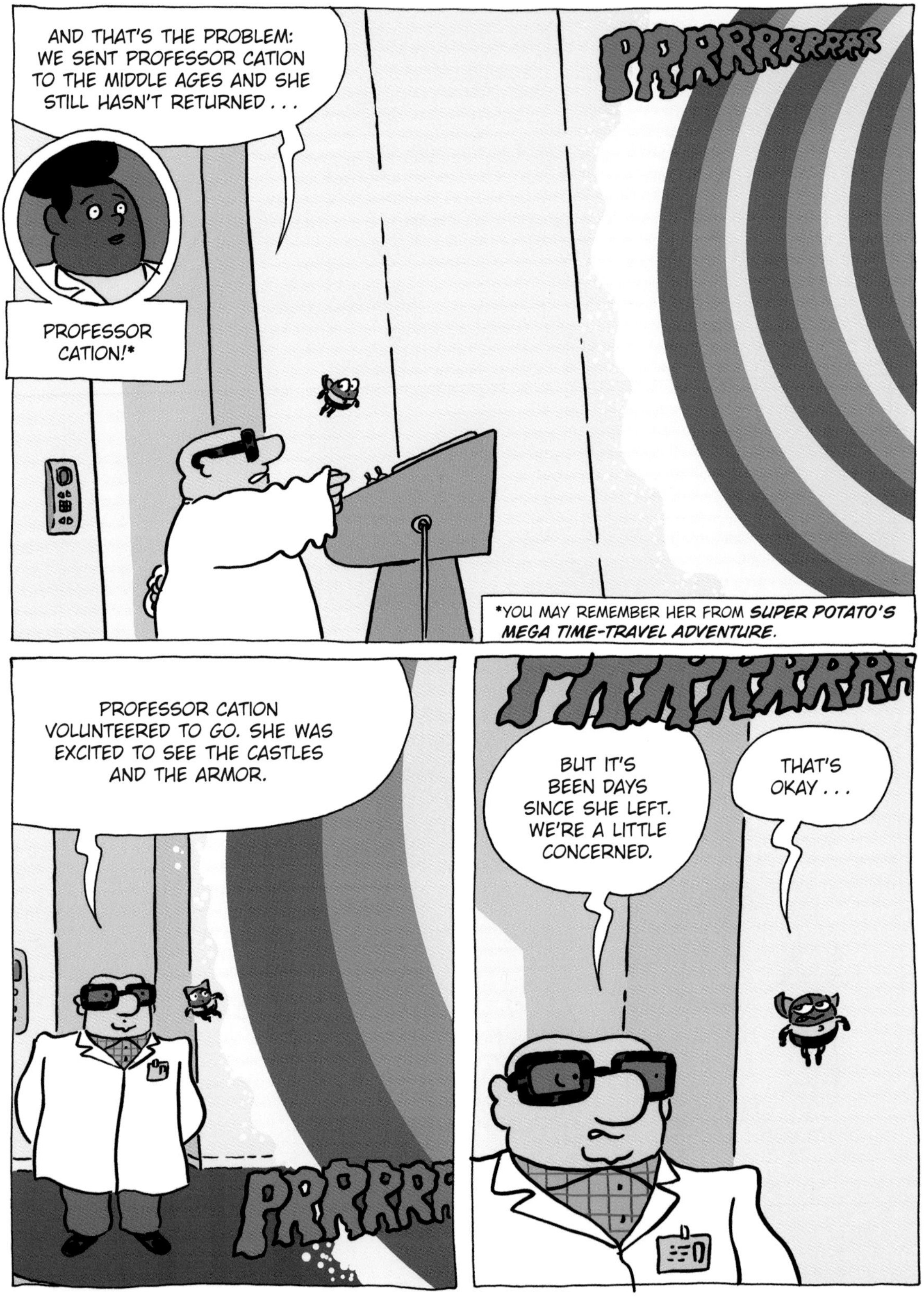
AND THAT'S THE PROBLEM: WE SENT PROFESSOR CATION TO THE MIDDLE AGES AND SHE STILL HASN'T RETURNED . . .
PRRRRRRRRAR
PROFESSOR CATION!*
*YOU MAY REMEMBER HER FROM SUPER POTATO'S MEGA TIME-TRAVEL ADVENTURE.
PROFESSOR CATION VOLUNTEERED TO GO. SHE WAS EXCITED TO SEE THE CASTLES AND THE ARMOR.
PRRRRR
BUT IT'S BEEN DAYS SINCE SHE LEFT. WE'RE A LITTLE CONCERNED.
THAT'S OKAY . . .

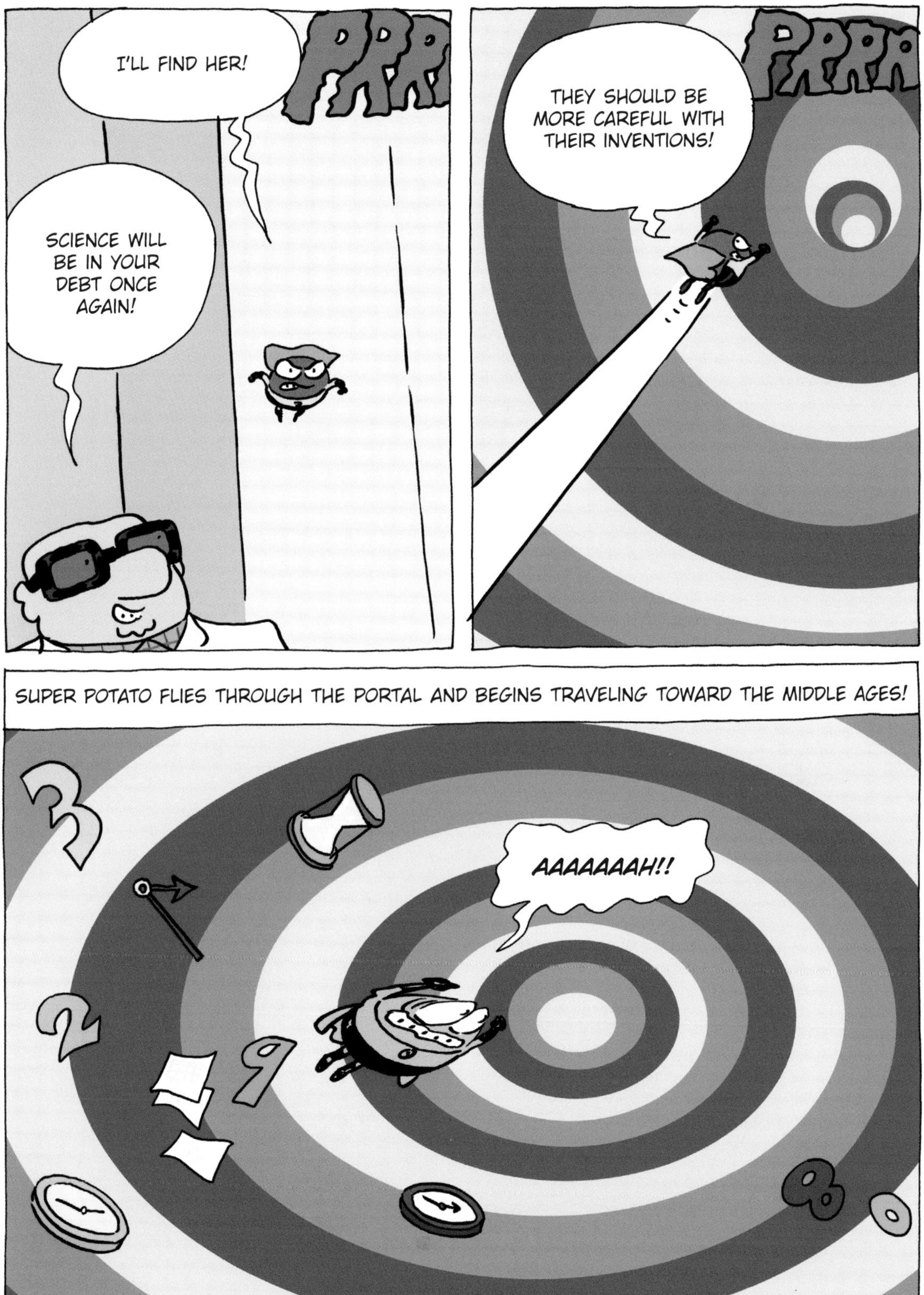
I'LL FIND HER!
SCIENCE WILL BE IN YOUR DEBT ONCE AGAIN!
THEY SHOULD BE MORE CAREFUL WITH THEIR INVENTIONS!
SUPER POTATO FLIES THROUGH THE PORTAL AND BEGINS TRAVELING TOWARD THE MIDDLE AGES!
AAAAAAAH!!

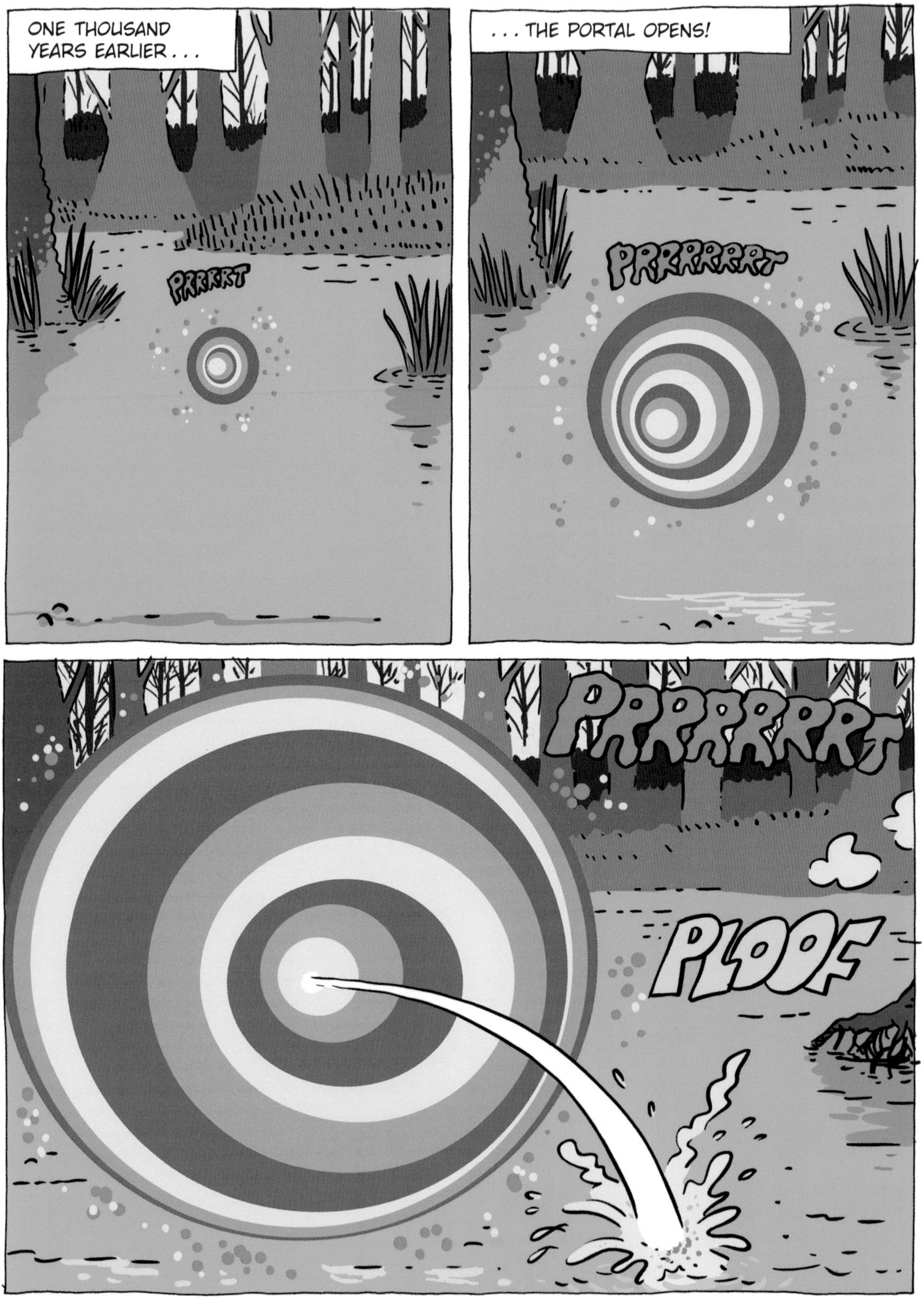
ONE THOUSAND YEARS EARLIER . . .
PRRRRT
. . . THE PORTAL OPENS!
PRRRRRRT
PRRRRRRT
PLOOF

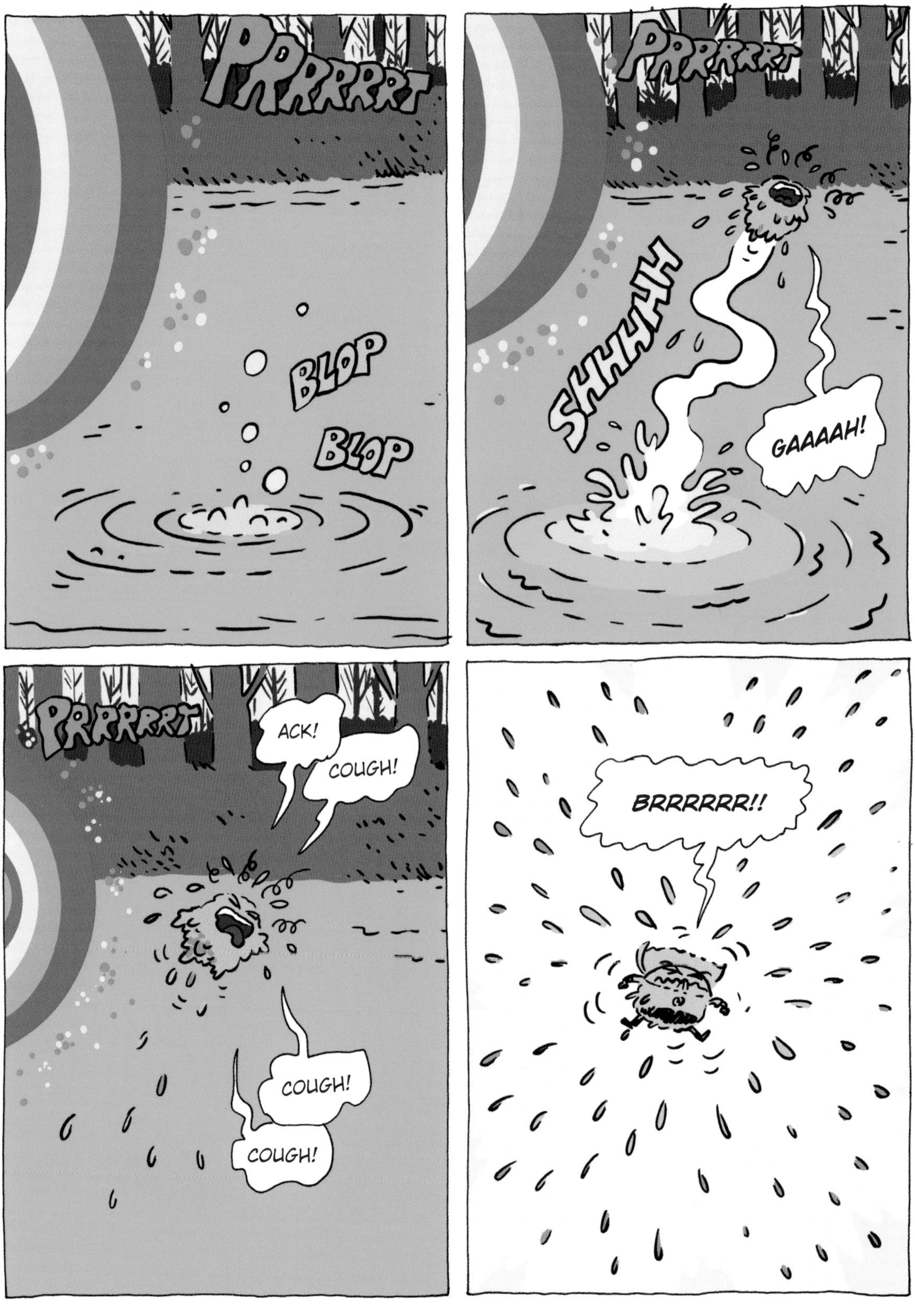
PRRRRRRT
BLOP
BLOP
PRRRRRT
SHHHHH
GAAAAH!
PRRRRRT
ACK!
COUGH!
COUGH!
COUGH!
BRRRRRR!!

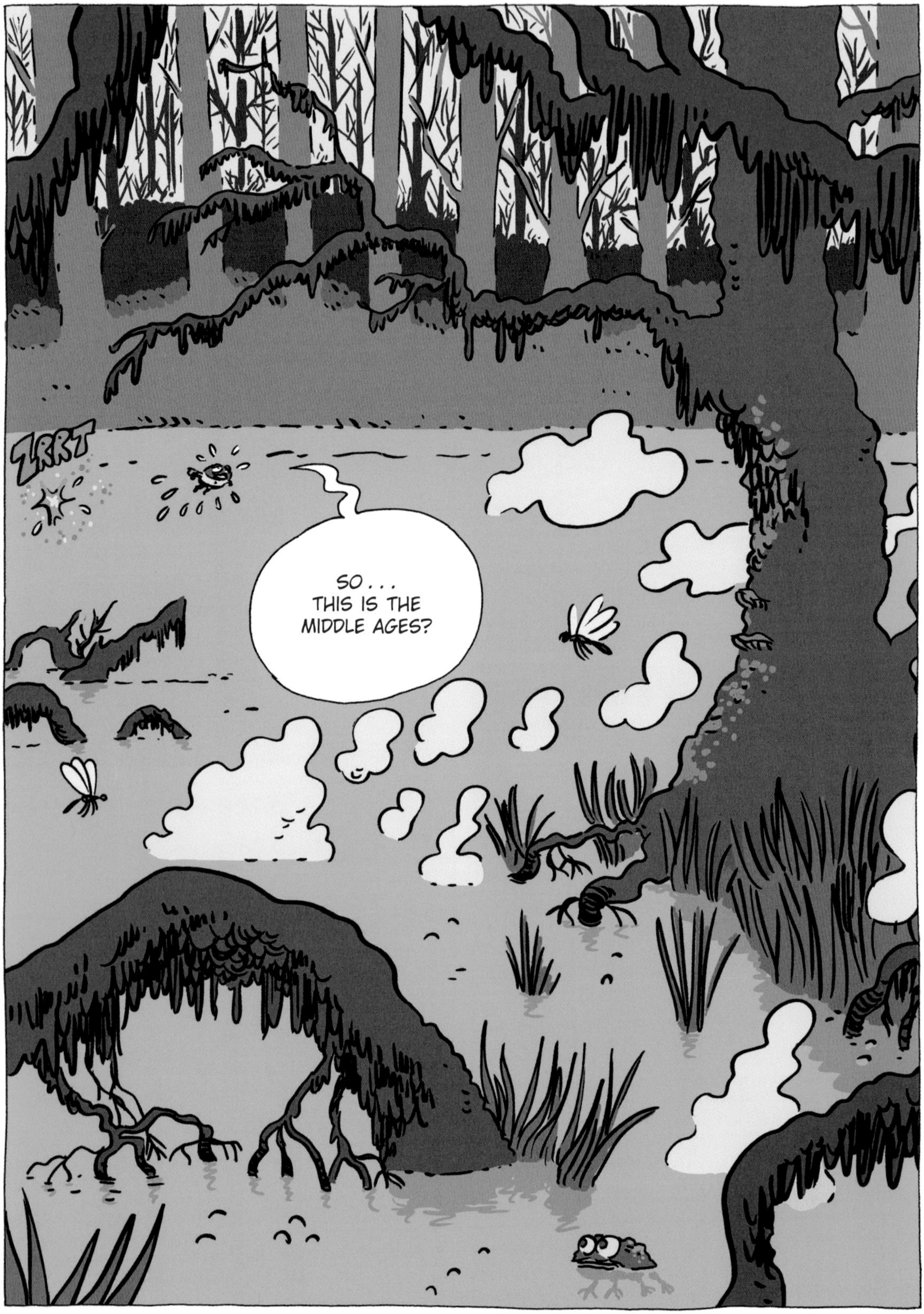
ZRRT
SO . . .
THIS IS THE
MIDDLE AGES?

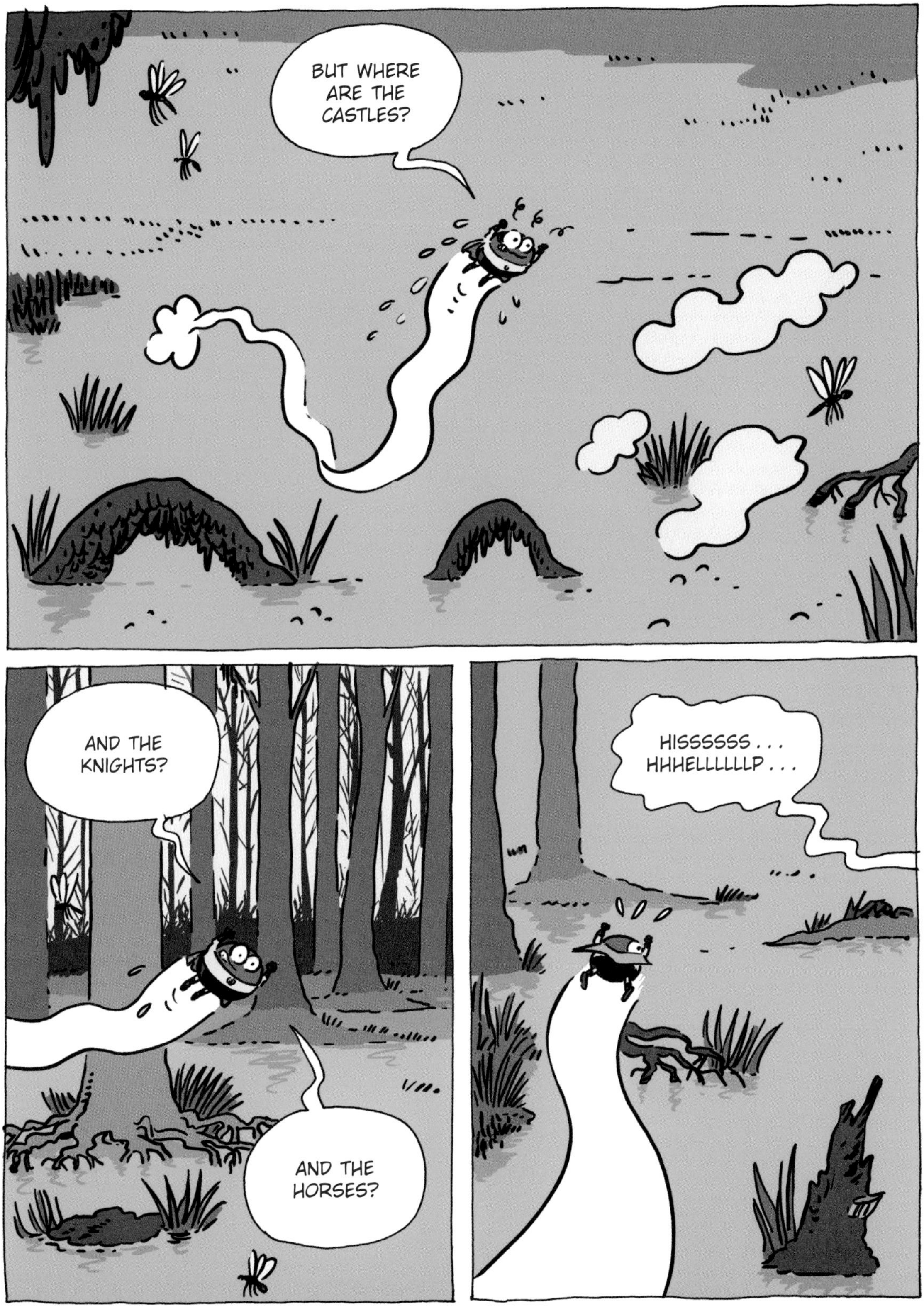
BUT WHERE ARE THE CASTLES?
AND THE KNIGHTS?
AND THE HORSES?
HISSSSSS . . . HHHELLLLLLLP . . .

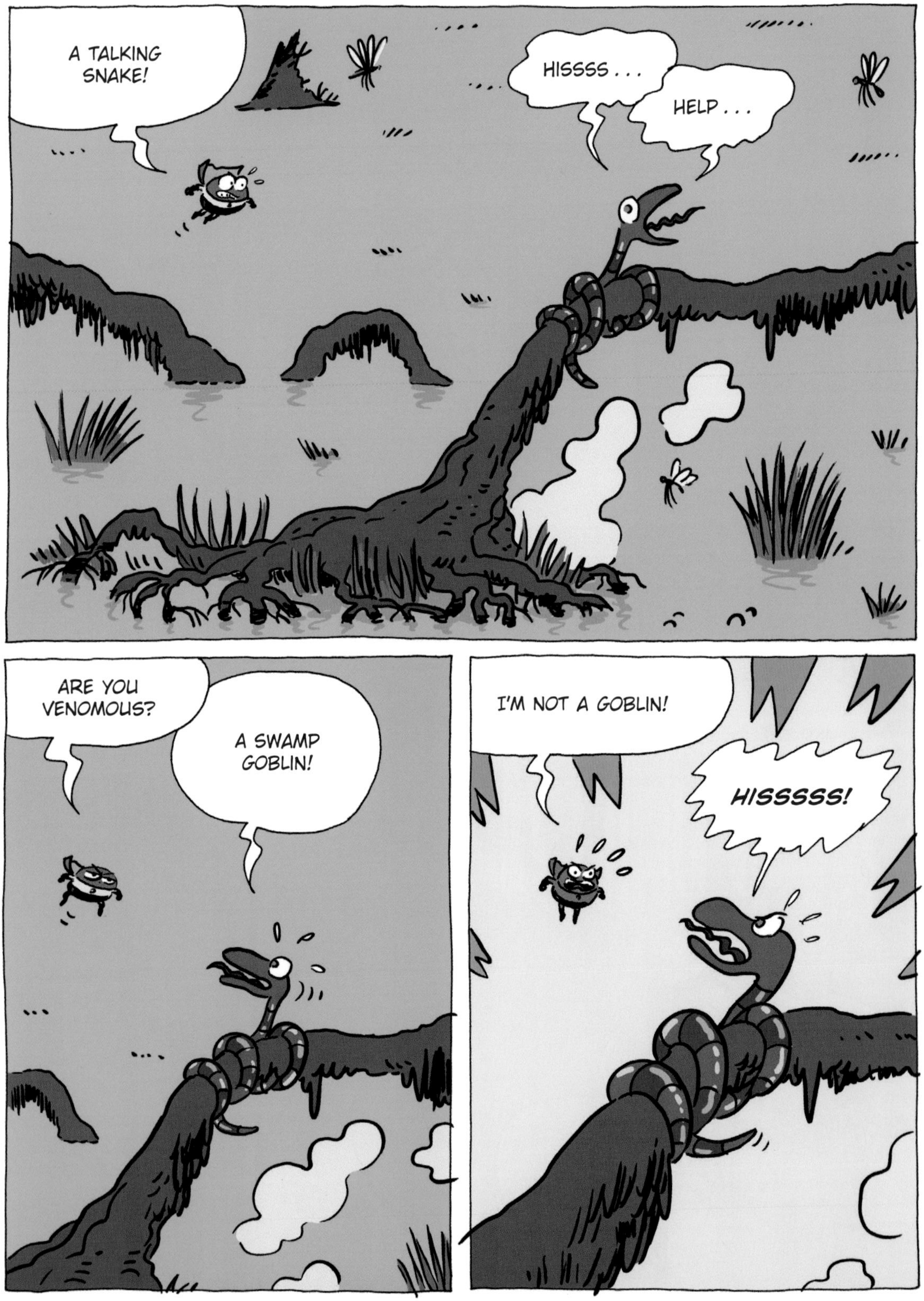
A TALKING SNAKE!
HISSSS . . .
HELP . . .
ARE YOU VENOMOUS?
A SWAMP GOBLIN!
I'M NOT A GOBLIN!
HISSSSS!

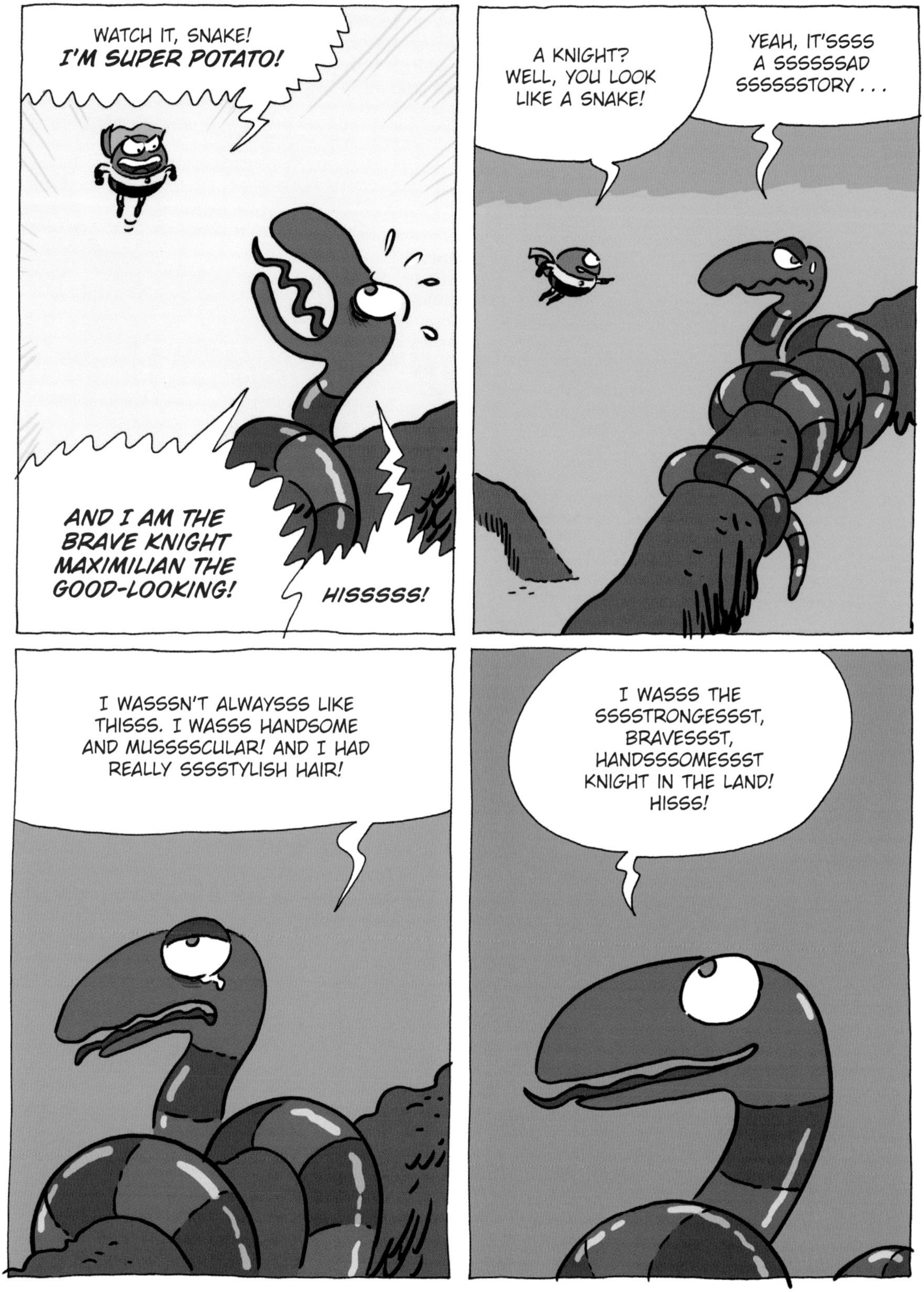
WATCH IT, SNAKE!
I'M SUPER POTATO!
AND I AM THE BRAVE KNIGHT MAXIMILIAN THE GOOD-LOOKING!
HISSSSS!
A KNIGHT? WELL, YOU LOOK LIKE A SNAKE!
YEAH, IT'SSSS A SSSSSSAD SSSSSSTORY . . .
I WASSSN'T ALWAYSSS LIKE THISSS. I WASSS HANDSOME AND MUSSSSCULAR! AND I HAD REALLY SSSSTYLISH HAIR!
I WASSS THE SSSSTRONGESSST, BRAVESSST, HANDSSSOMESSST KNIGHT IN THE LAND! HISSS!

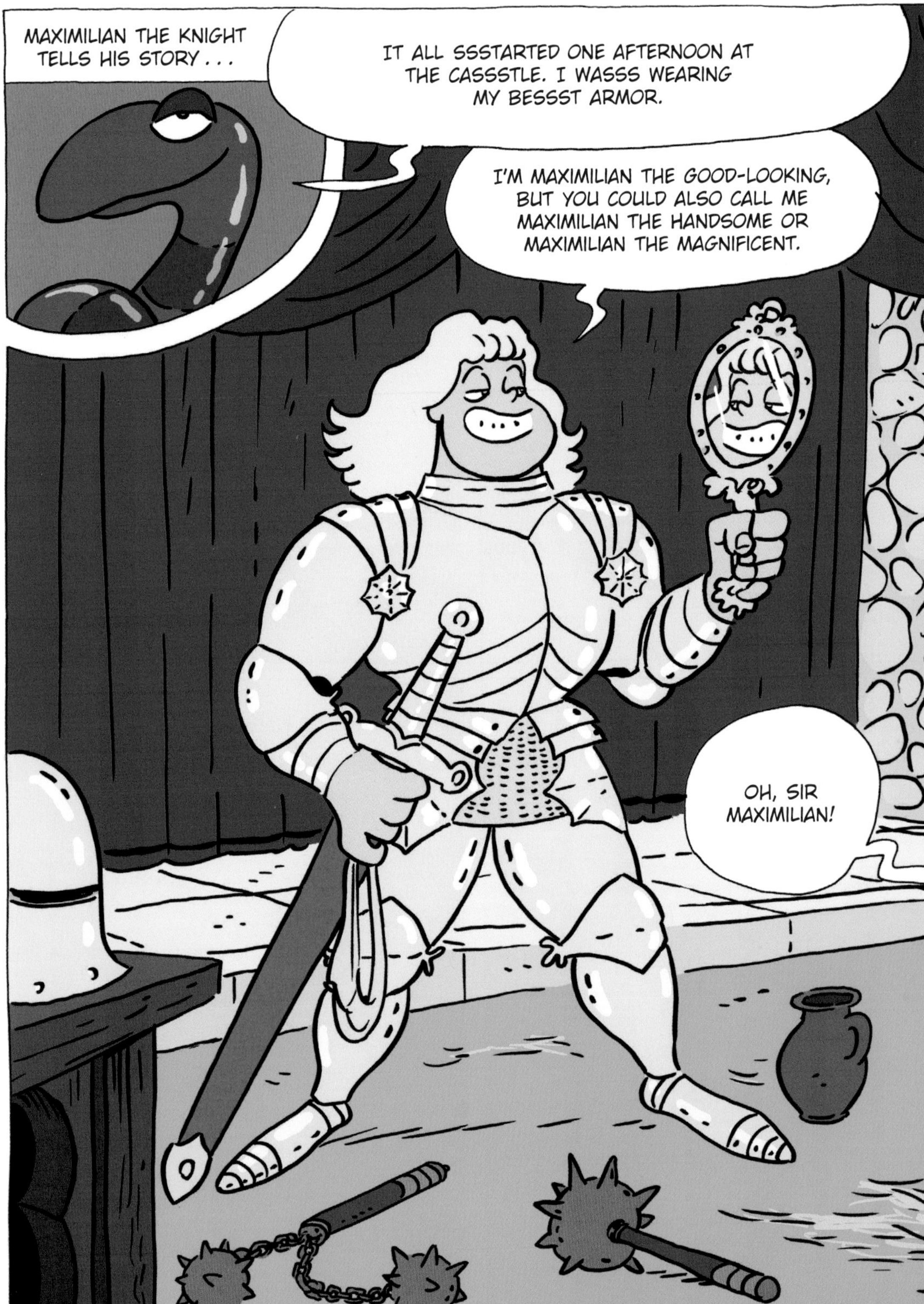
MAXIMILIAN THE KNIGHT TELLS HIS STORY . . .
IT ALL SSSTARTED ONE AFTERNOON AT THE CASSSTLE. I WASSS WEARING MY BESSST ARMOR.
I'M MAXIMILIAN THE GOOD-LOOKING, BUT YOU COULD ALSO CALL ME MAXIMILIAN THE HANDSOME OR MAXIMILIAN THE MAGNIFICENT.
OH, SIR MAXIMILIAN!

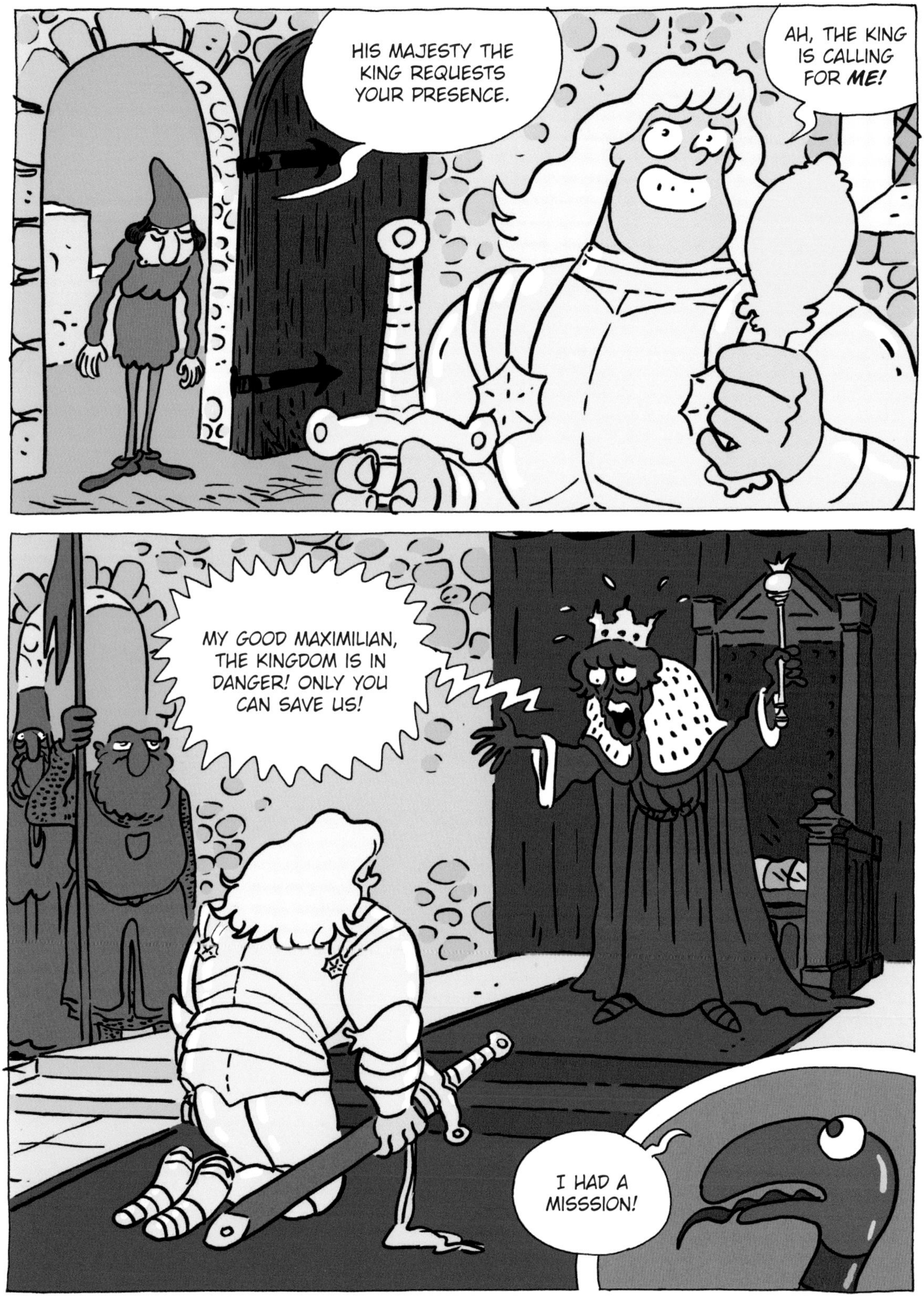
HIS MAJESTY THE KING REQUESTS YOUR PRESENCE.
AH, THE KING IS CALLING FOR *ME!*
MY GOOD MAXIMILIAN, THE KINGDOM IS IN DANGER! ONLY YOU CAN SAVE US!
I HAD A MISSSION!

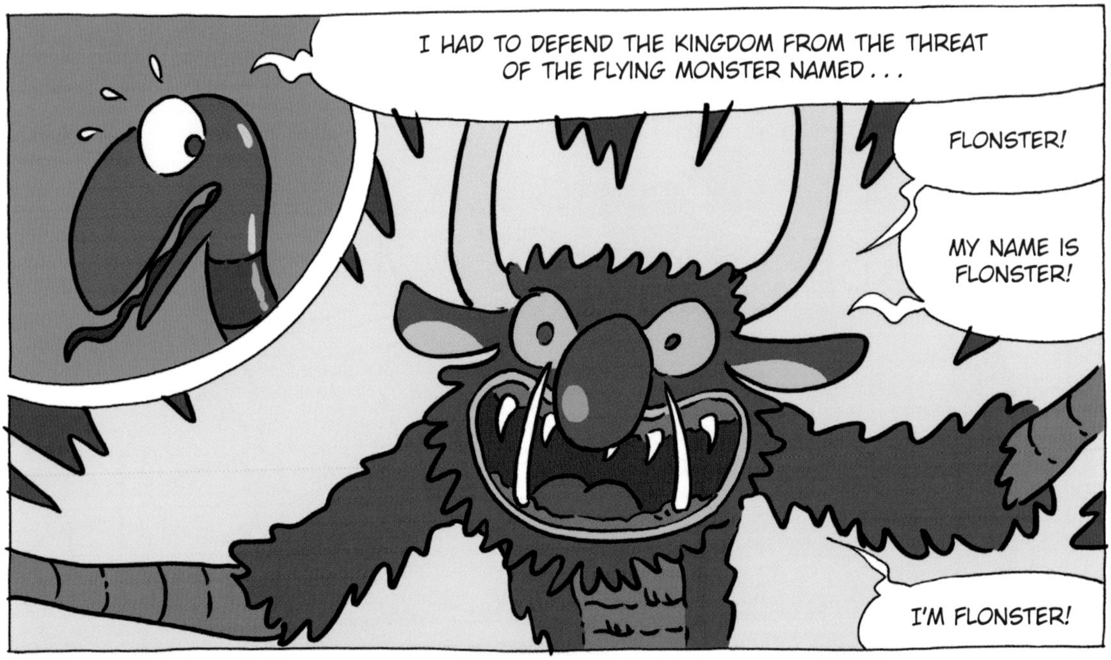
I HAD TO DEFEND THE KINGDOM FROM THE THREAT OF THE FLYING MONSTER NAMED . . .
FLONSTER!
MY NAME IS FLONSTER!
I'M FLONSTER!

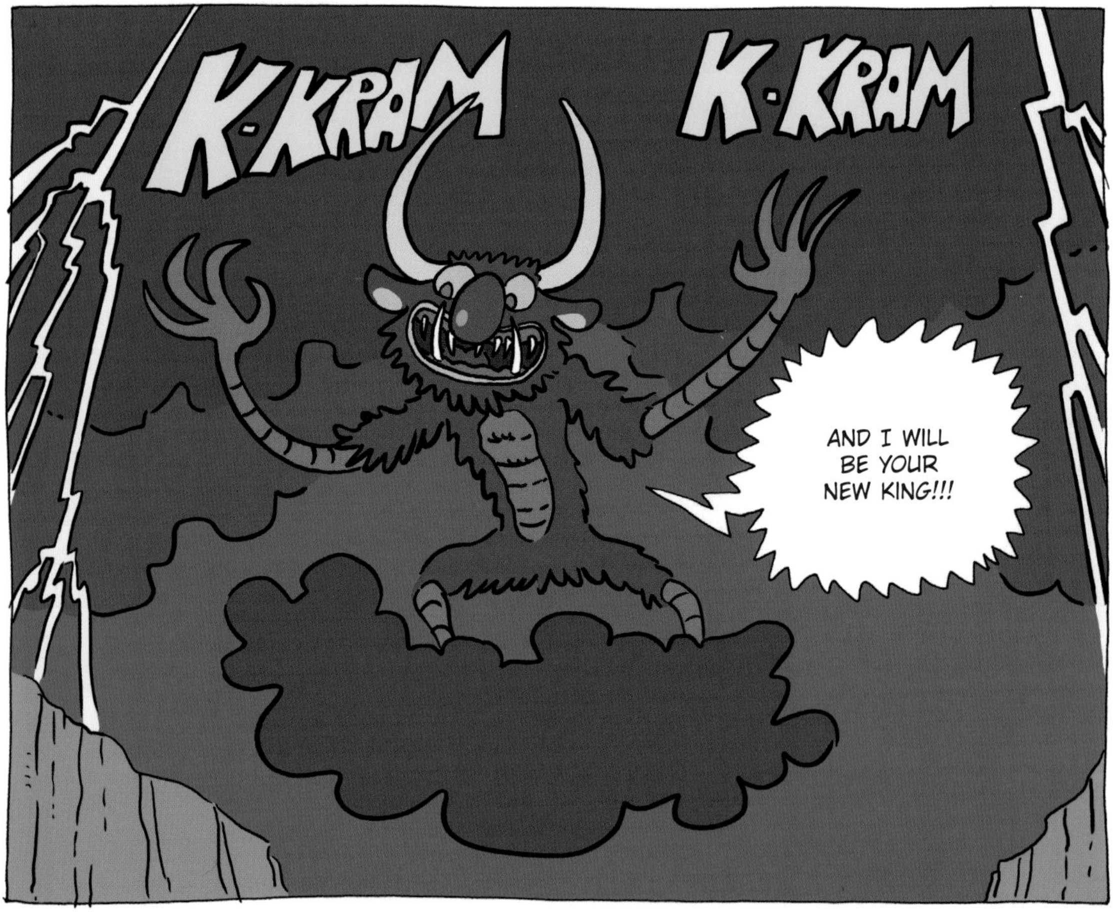
K-KRAM
K-KRAM
AND I WILL BE YOUR NEW KING!!!

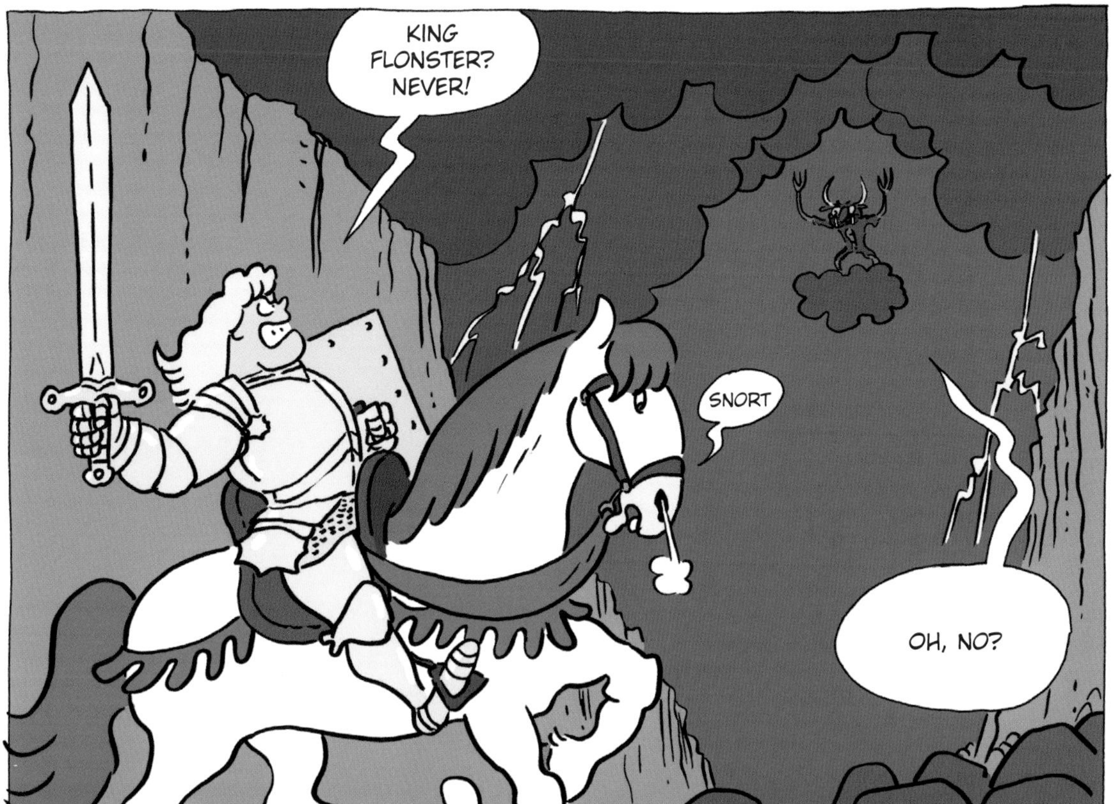
KING FLONSTER? NEVER!
SNORT
OH, NO?

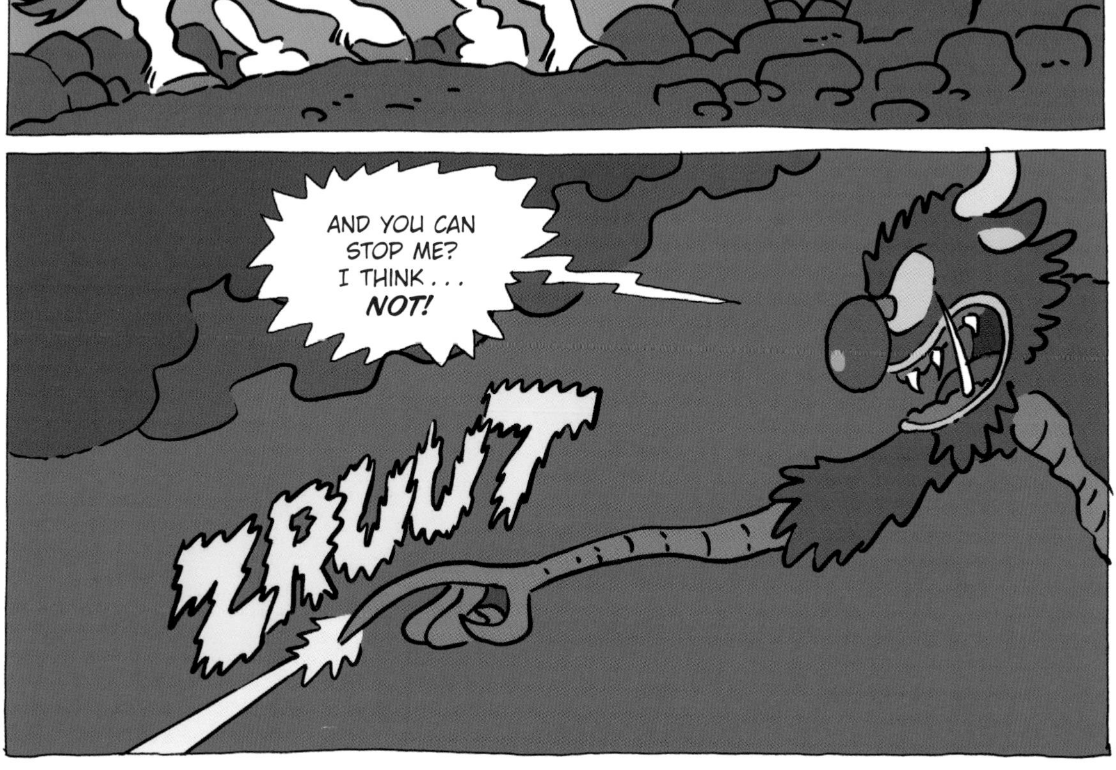
AND YOU CAN STOP ME? I THINK . . . **NOT!**
ZRUUT

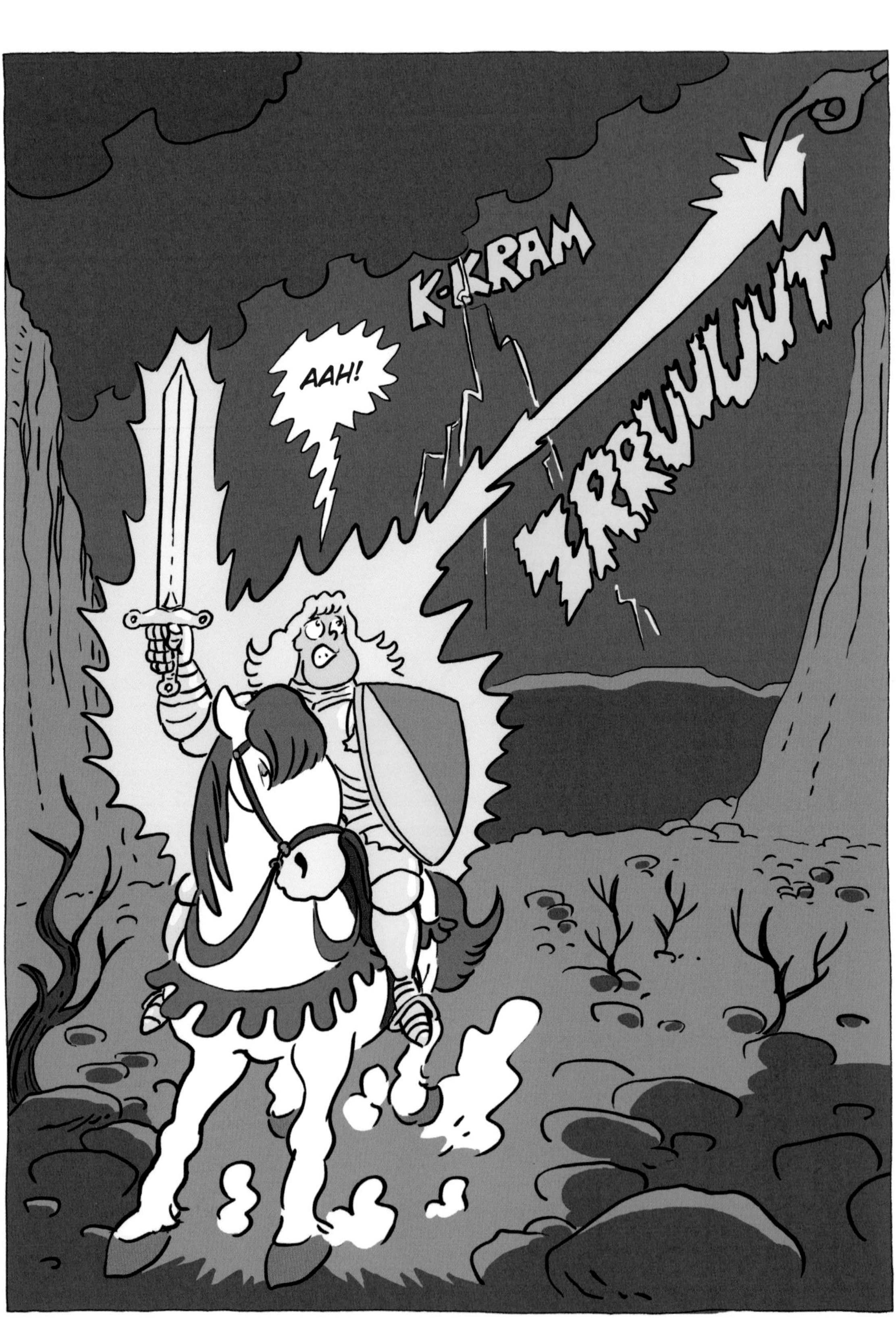
AAH!
K-KRAM
ZRRUUUUT

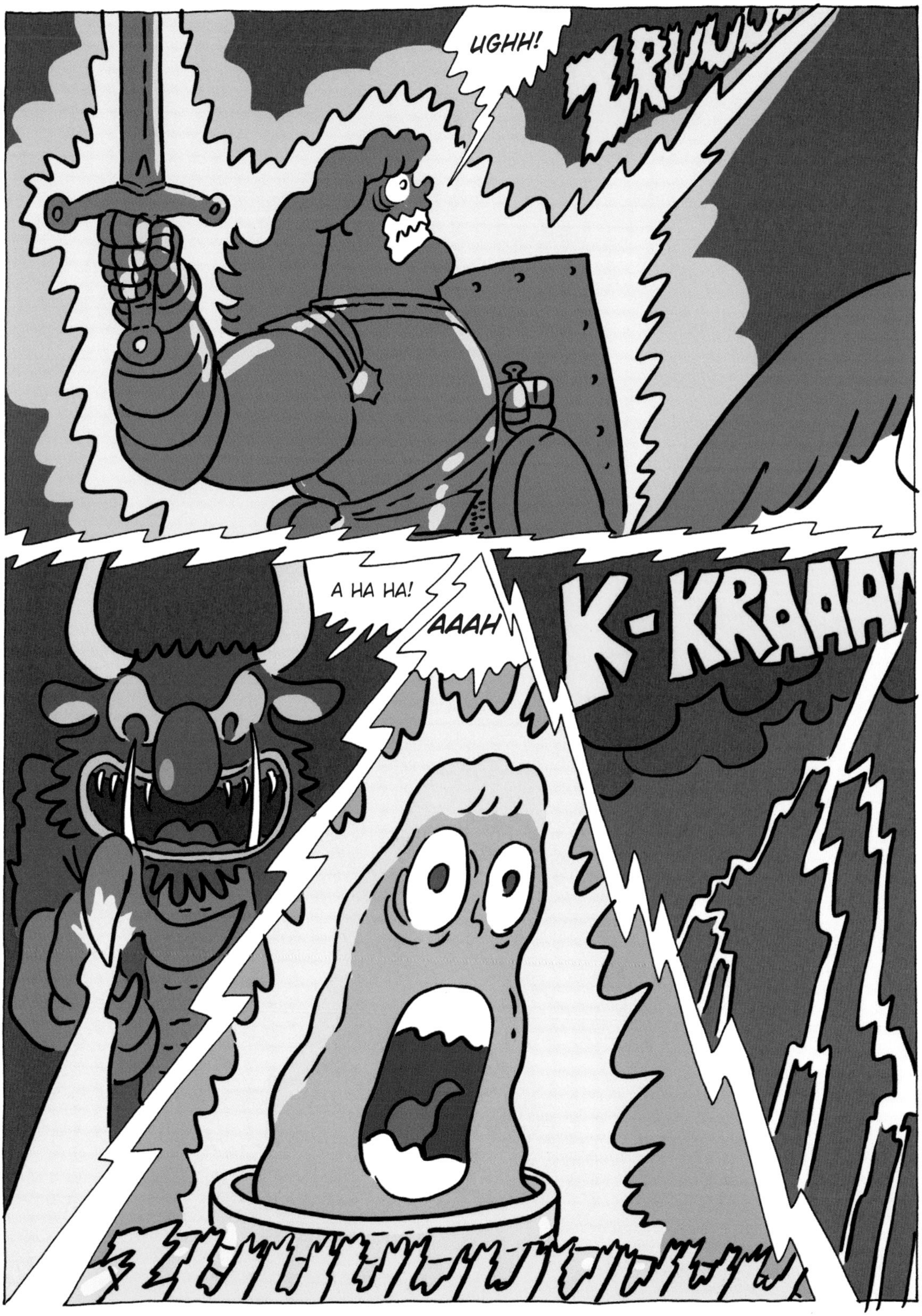
UGHH!
ZRUU
A HA HA!
AAAH
K-KRAAA

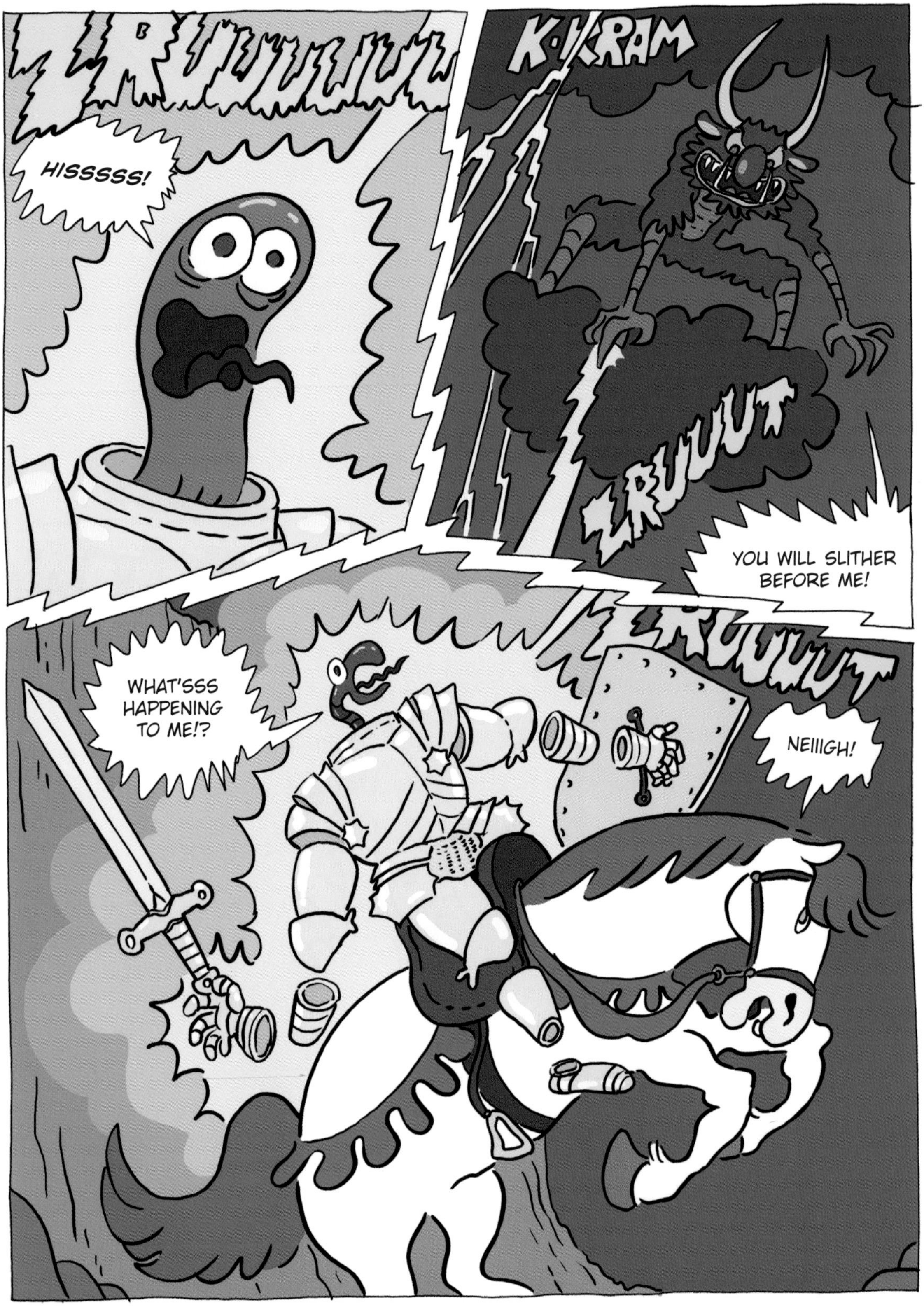
ZRUUUUUUUT
HISSSSS!
K-KRAM
ZRUUUT
YOU WILL SLITHER BEFORE ME!
ZRUUUUT
WHAT'SSS HAPPENING TO ME!?
NEIIIGH!

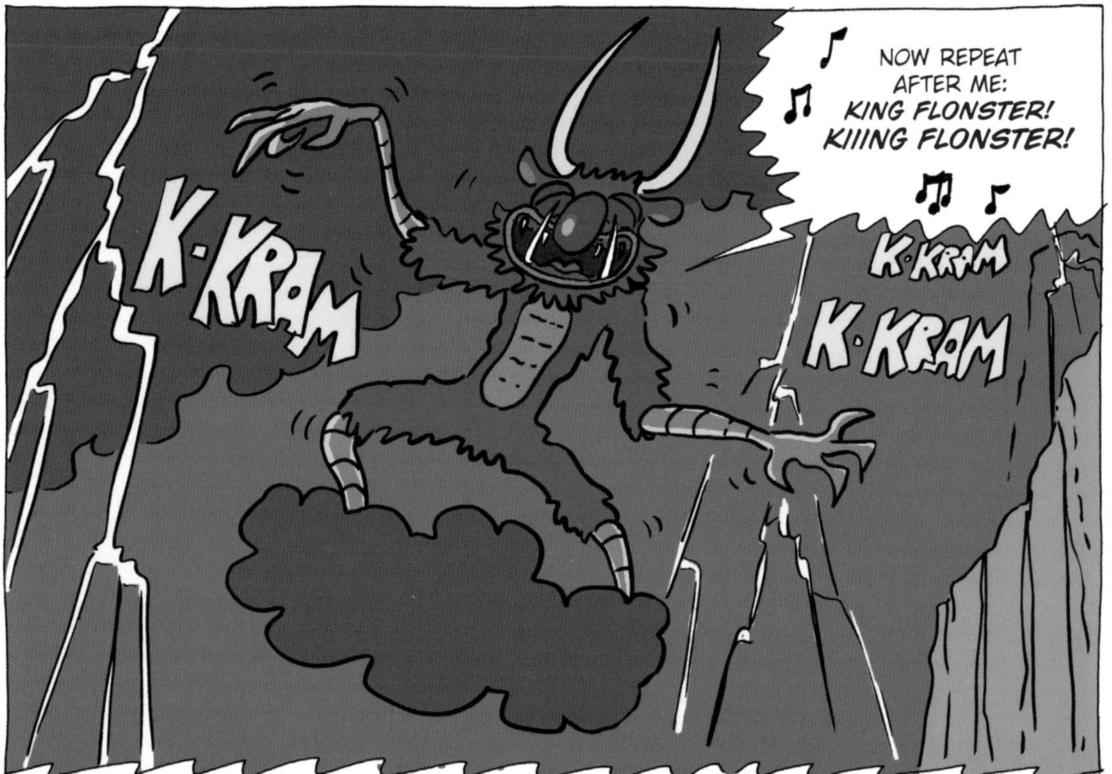
NOW REPEAT AFTER ME: KING FLONSTER! KIIING FLONSTER!
K-KRAM
K-KRAM
K-KRAM
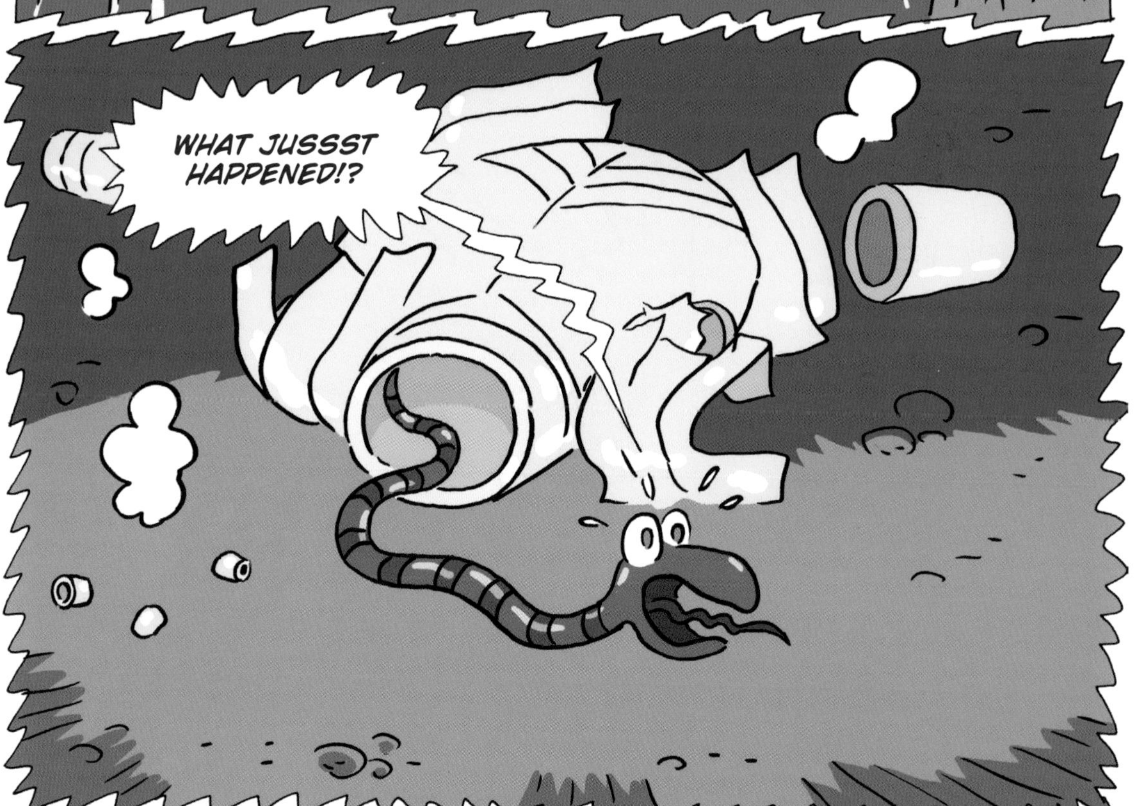
WHAT JUSSST HAPPENED!?

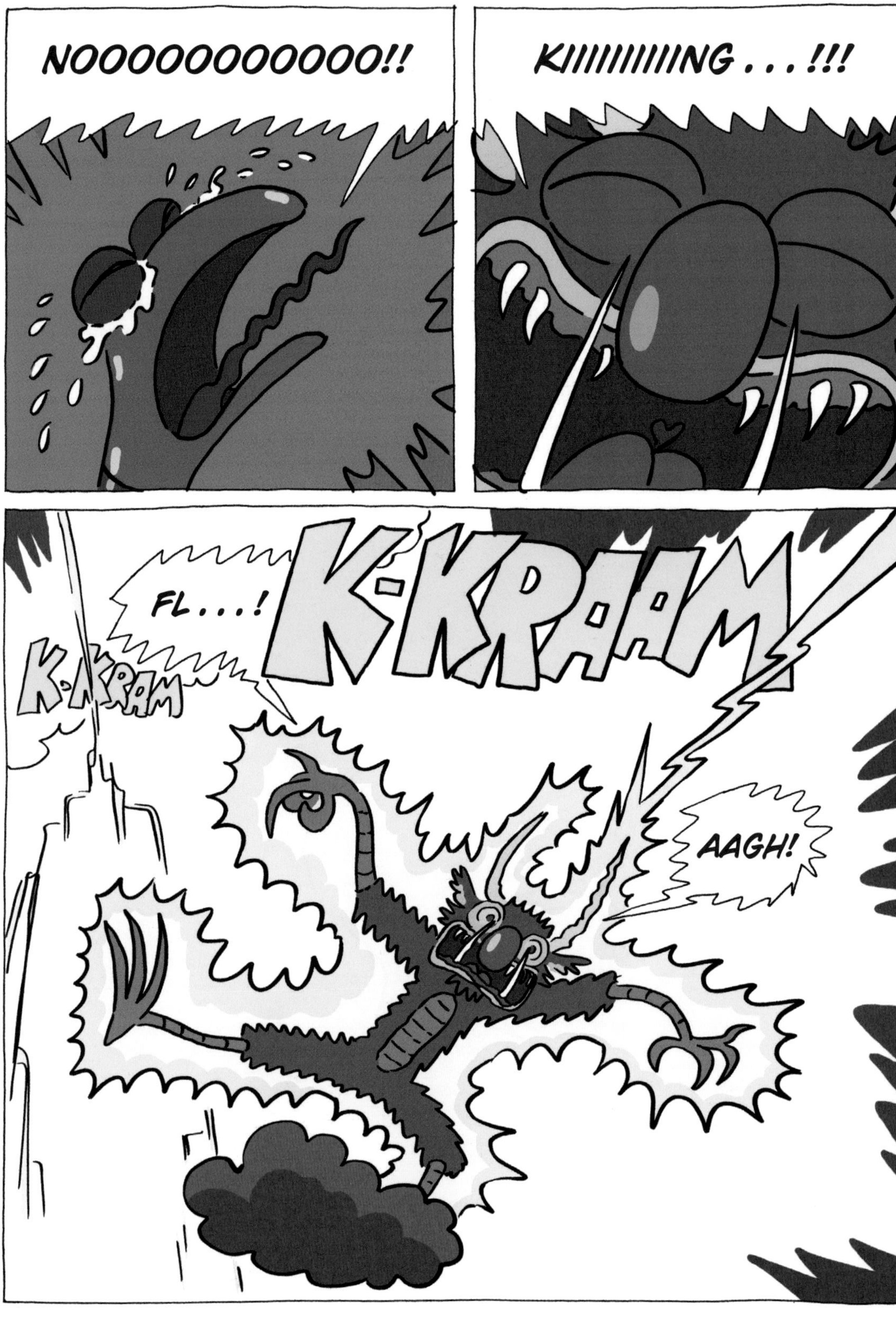
NOOOOOOOOOOOO!!
KIIIIIIIIIING . . . !!!
FL . . . !
K-KRAAM
K-KRAAM
AAGH!

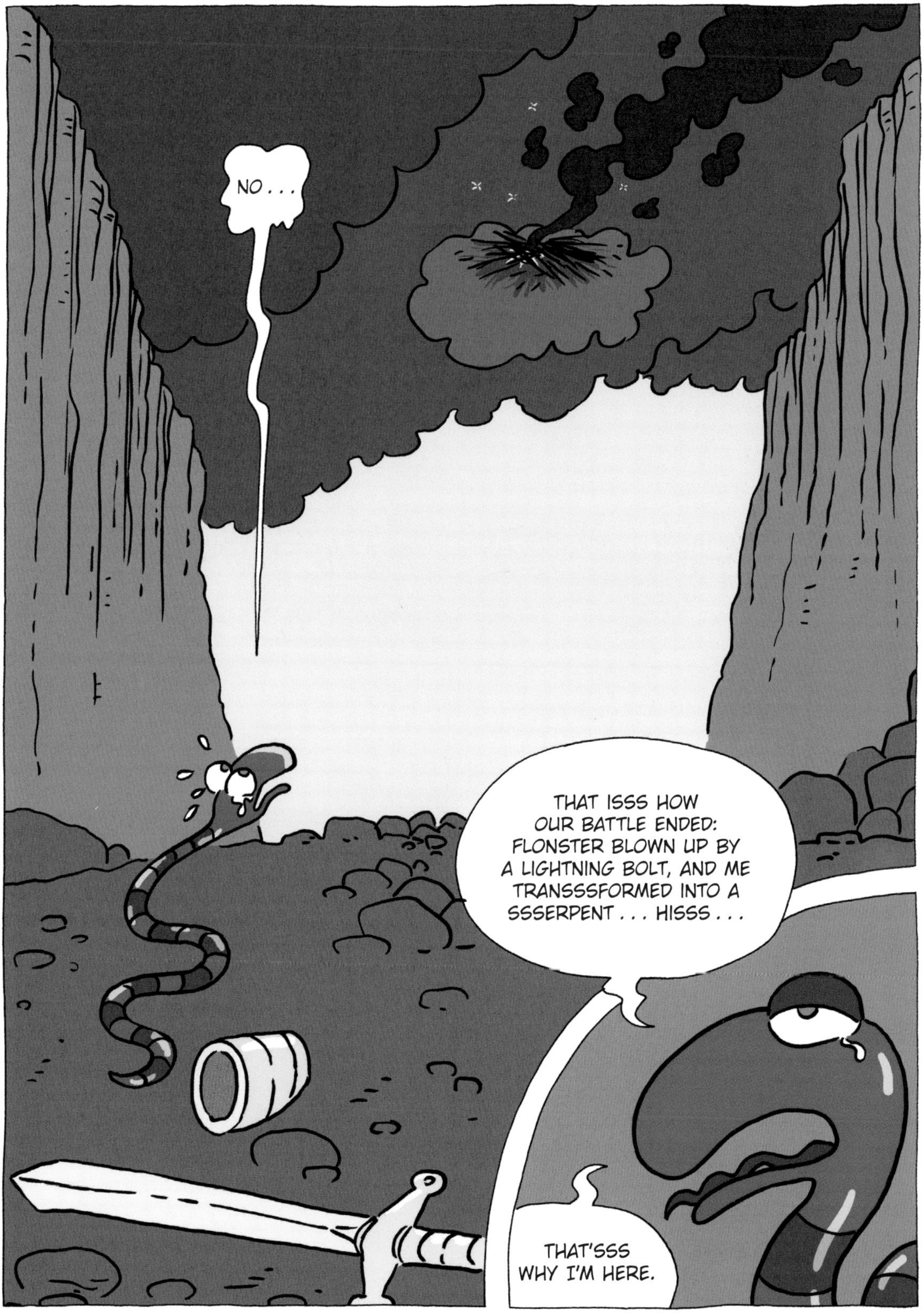
NO . . .
THAT ISSS HOW OUR BATTLE ENDED: FLONSTER BLOWN UP BY A LIGHTNING BOLT, AND ME TRANSSSFORMED INTO A SSSERPENT . . . HISSS . . .
THAT'SSS WHY I'M HERE.

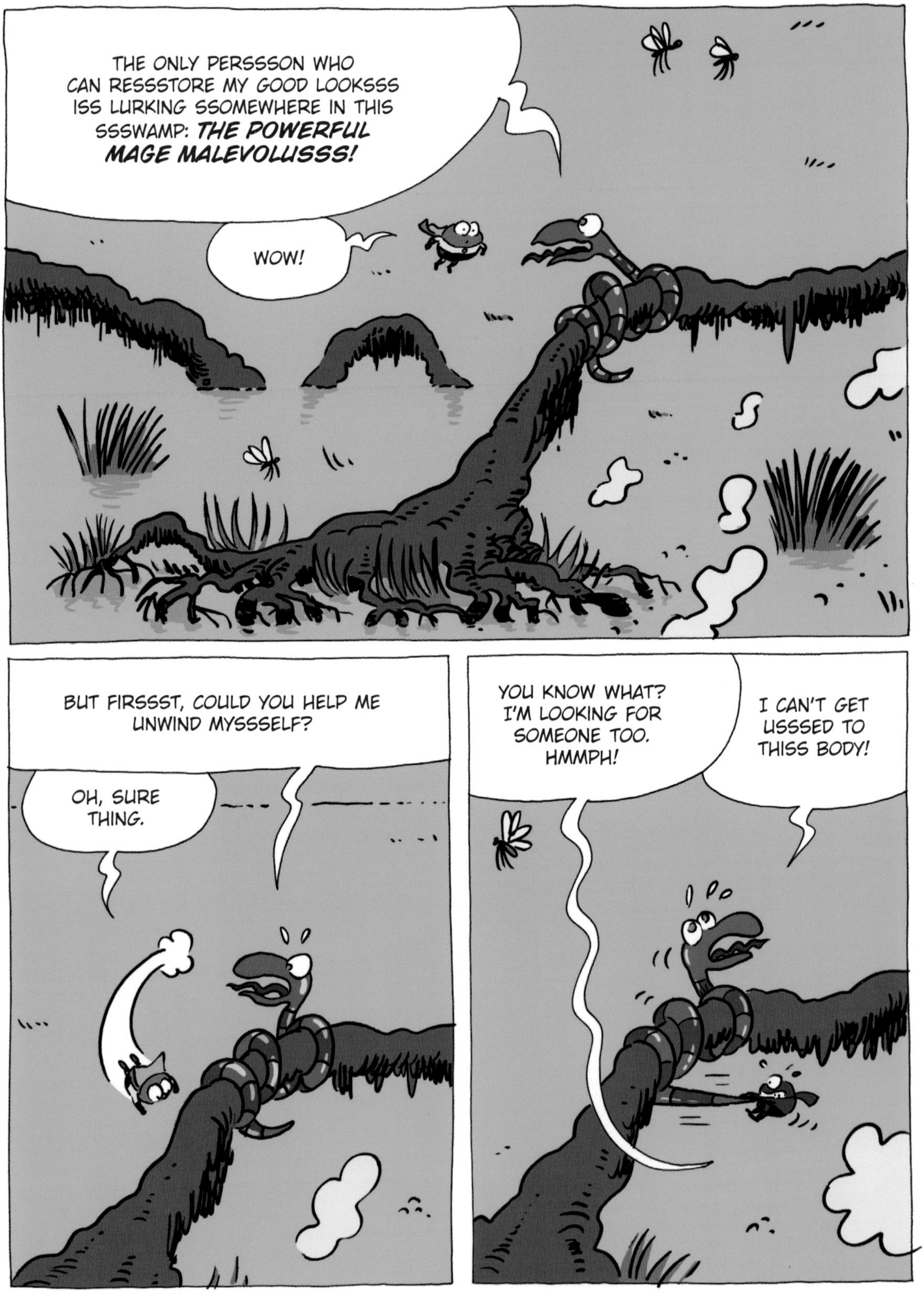
THE ONLY PERSSSON WHO CAN RESSSTORE MY GOOD LOOKSSS ISS LURKING SSOMEWHERE IN THIS SSSWAMP: ***THE POWERFUL MAGE MALEVOLUSSS!***
WOW!
BUT FIRSSST, COULD YOU HELP ME UNWIND MYSSSELF?
OH, SURE THING.
YOU KNOW WHAT? I'M LOOKING FOR SOMEONE TOO. HMMPH!
I CAN'T GET USSED TO THISS BODY!

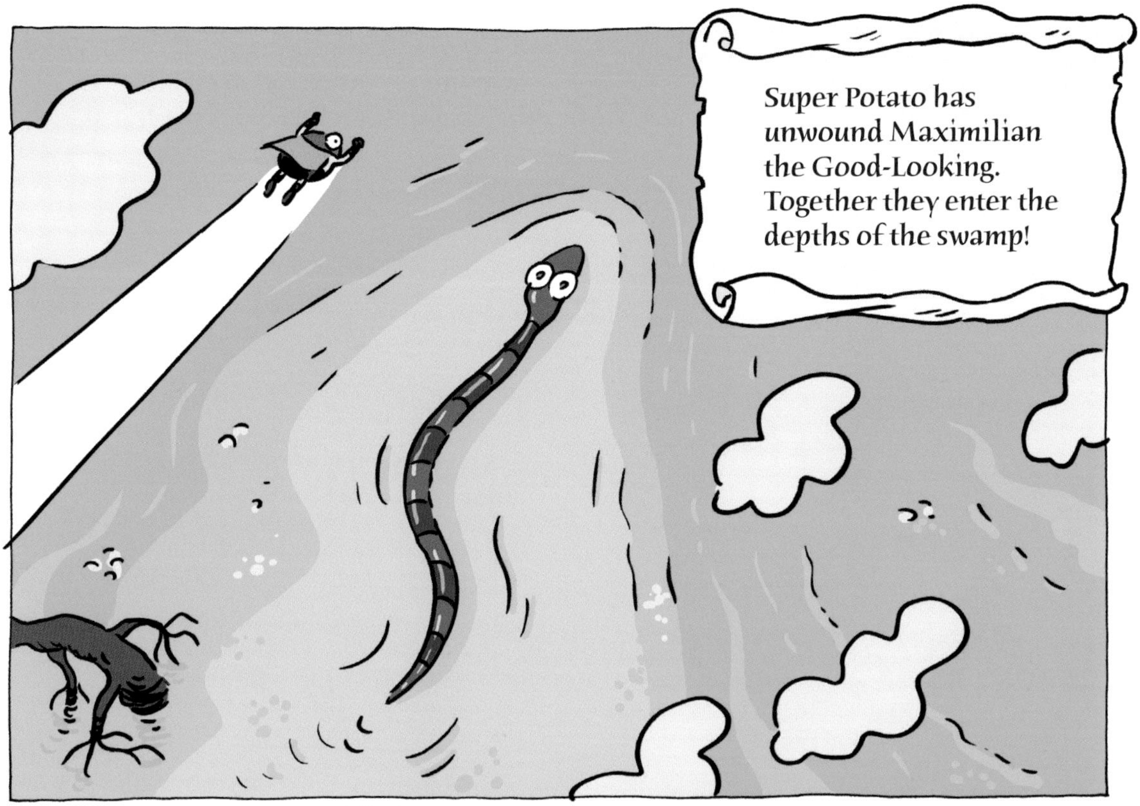
Super Potato has unwound Maximilian the Good-Looking. Together they enter the depths of the swamp!

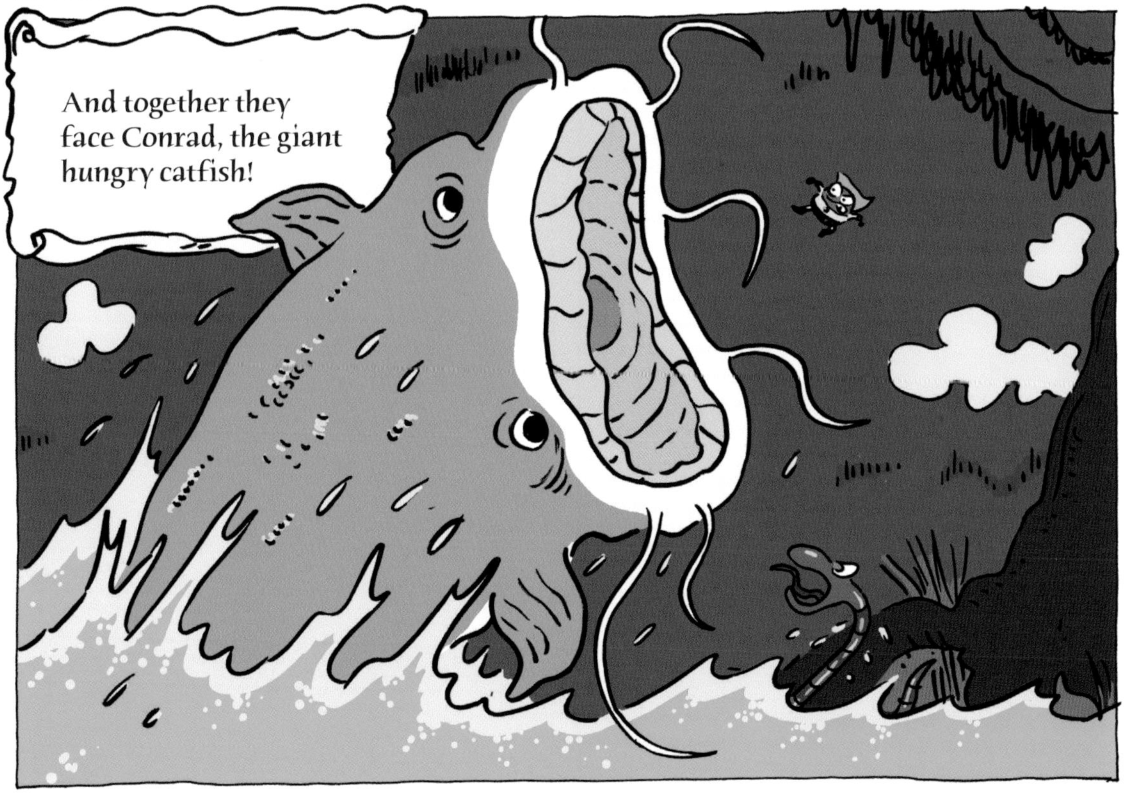
And together they face Conrad, the giant hungry catfish!

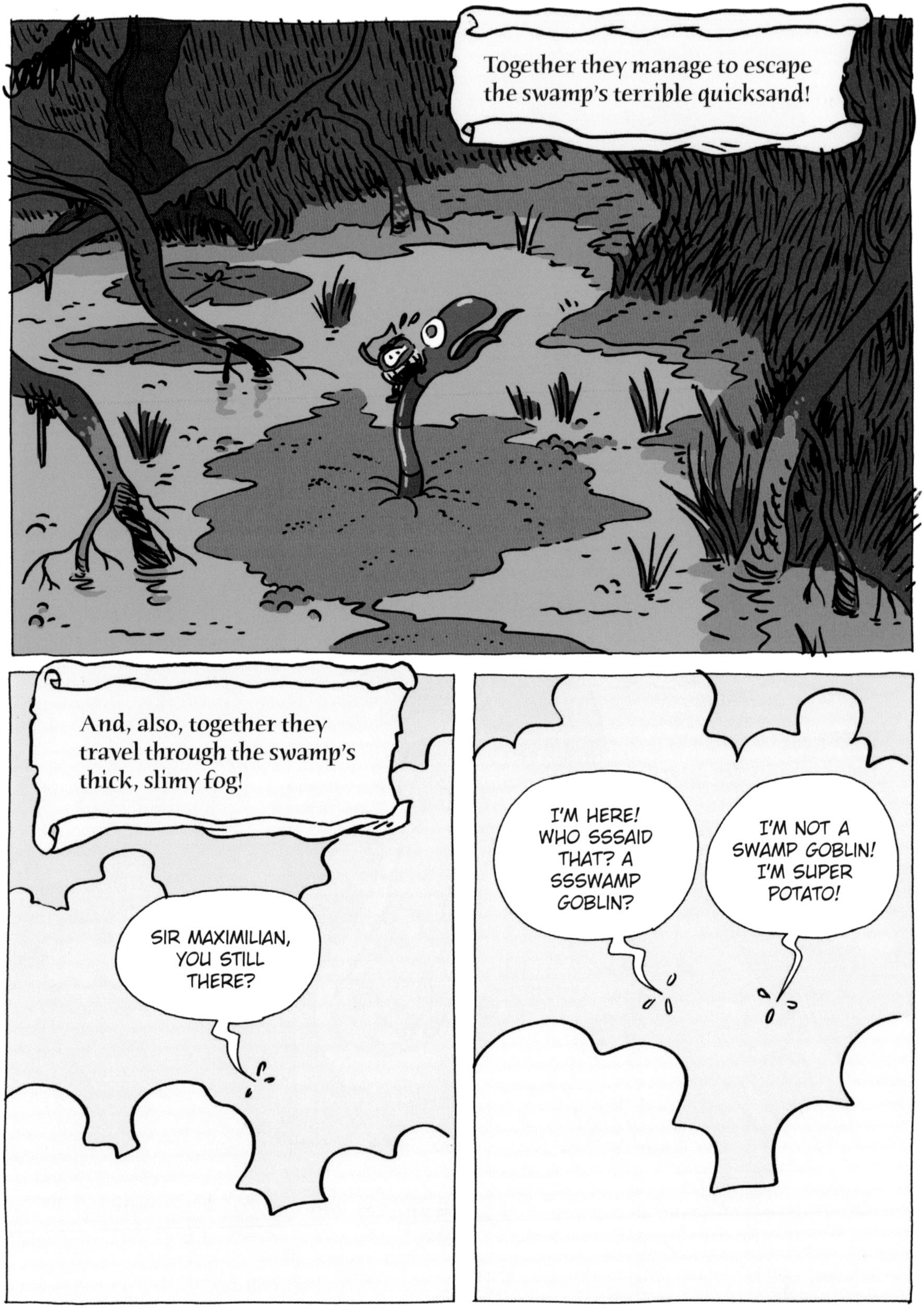
Together they manage to escape the swamp's terrible quicksand!
And, also, together they travel through the swamp's thick, slimy fog!
SIR MAXIMILIAN, YOU STILL THERE?
I'M HERE! WHO SSSAID THAT? A SSSWAMP GOBLIN?
I'M NOT A SWAMP GOBLIN! I'M SUPER POTATO!

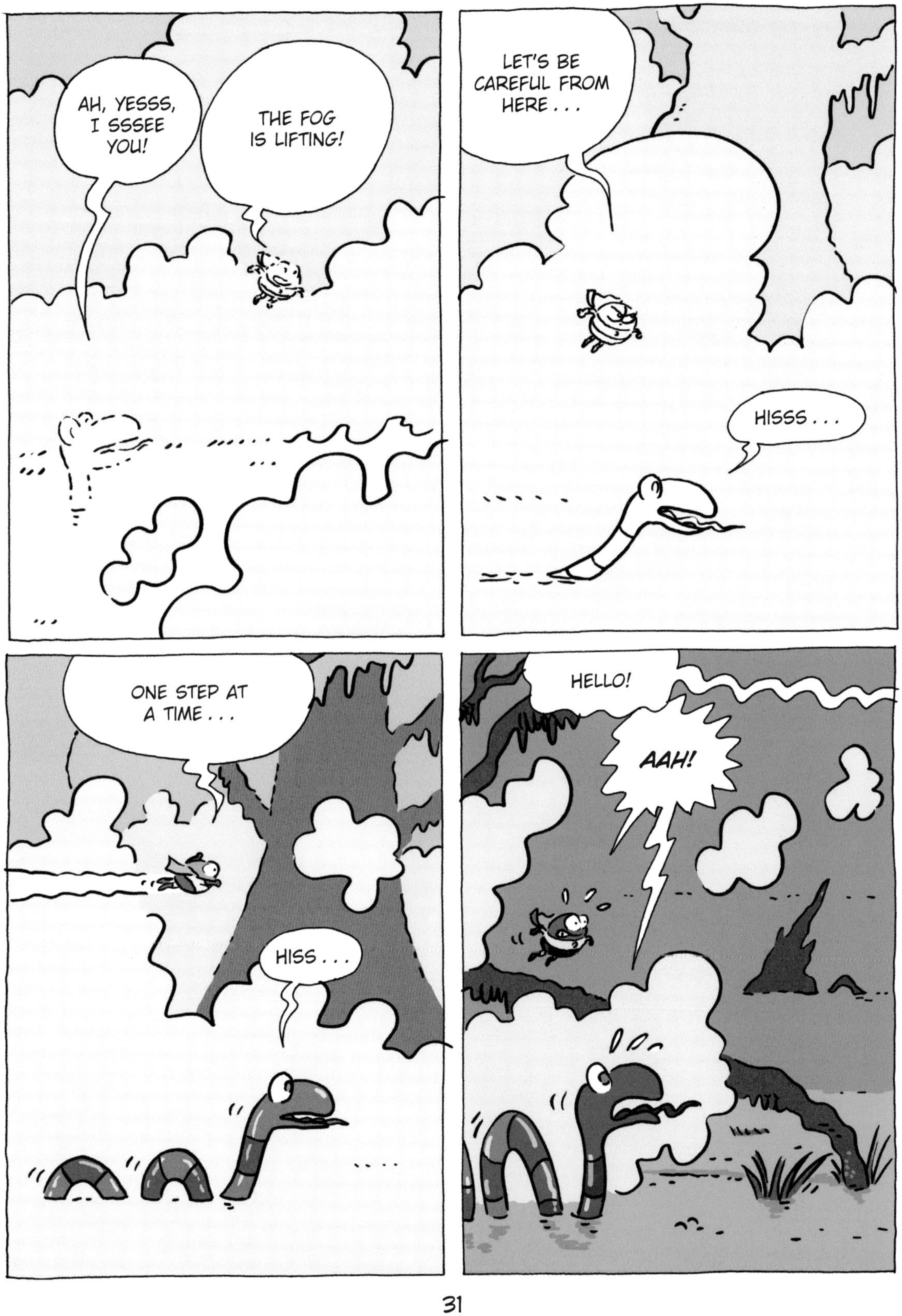
AH, YESSS, I SSSEE YOU!
THE FOG IS LIFTING!
LET'S BE CAREFUL FROM HERE . . .
HISSS . . .
ONE STEP AT A TIME . . .
HISS . . .
HELLO!
AAH!

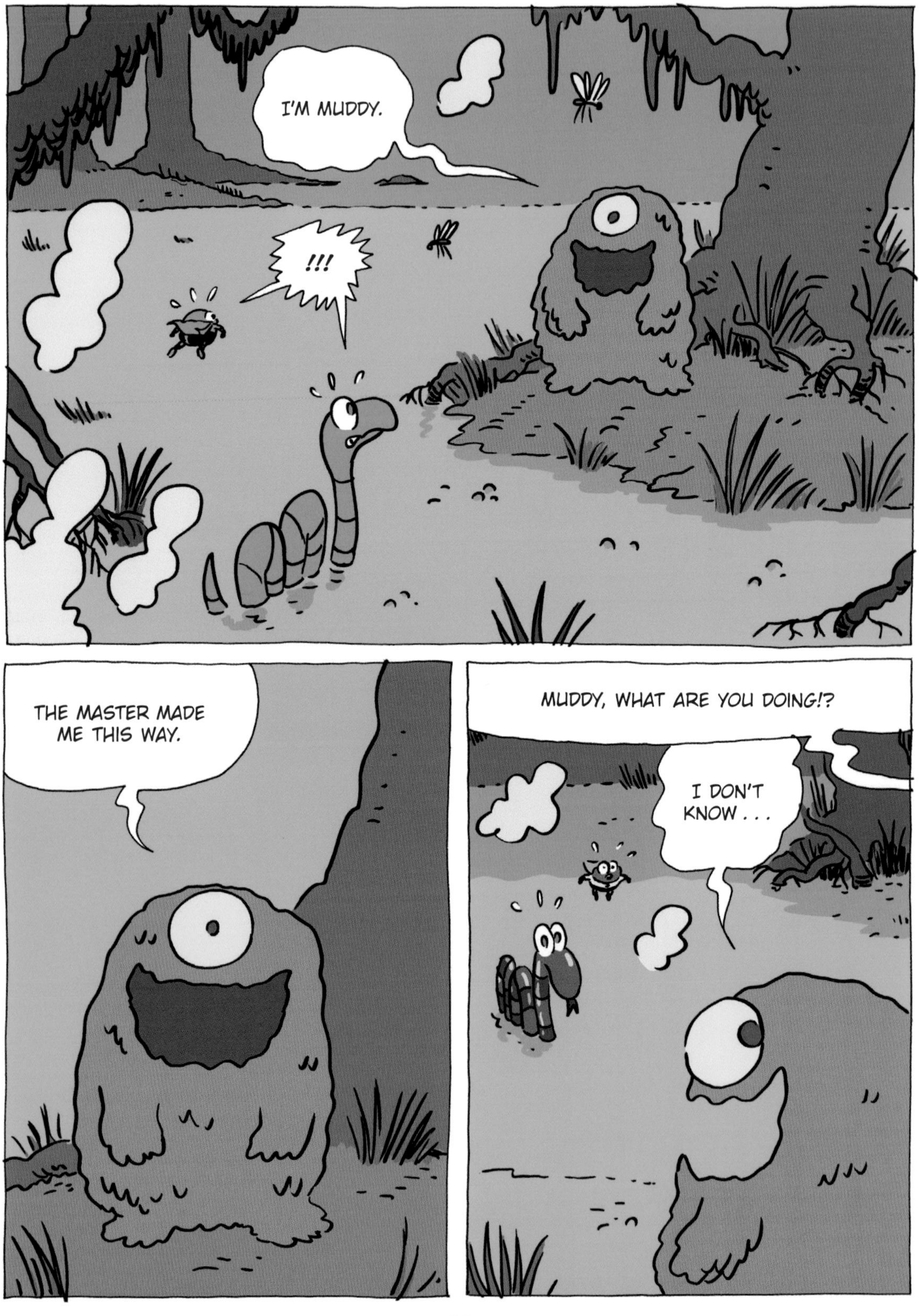
I'M MUDDY.
!!!
THE MASTER MADE ME THIS WAY.
MUDDY, WHAT ARE YOU DOING!?
I DON'T KNOW . . .

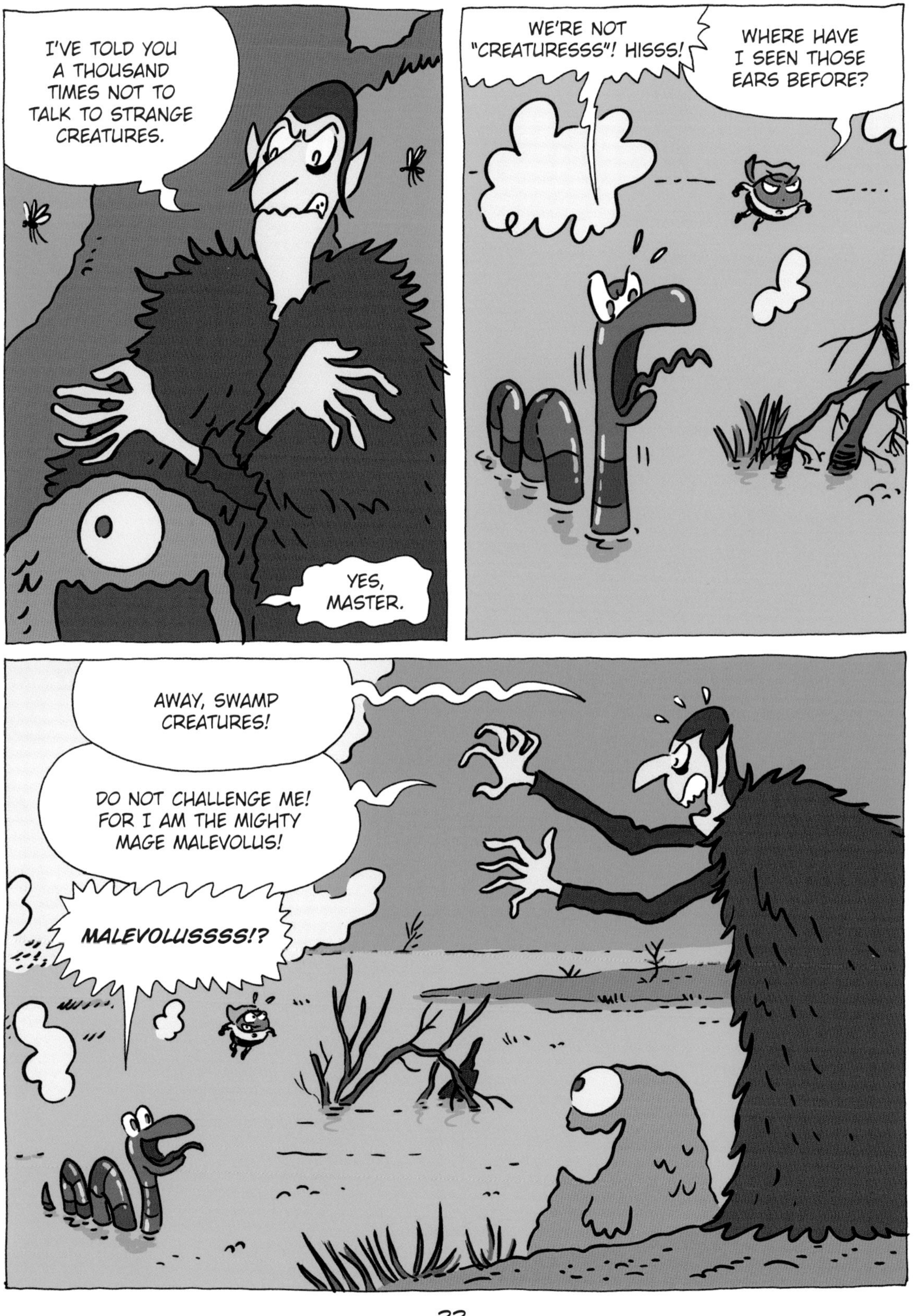
I'VE TOLD YOU A THOUSAND TIMES NOT TO TALK TO STRANGE CREATURES.
YES, MASTER.
WE'RE NOT "CREATURESSS"! HISSS!
WHERE HAVE I SEEN THOSE EARS BEFORE?
AWAY, SWAMP CREATURES!
DO NOT CHALLENGE ME! FOR I AM THE MIGHTY MAGE MALEVOLUS!
MALEVOLUSSSS!?

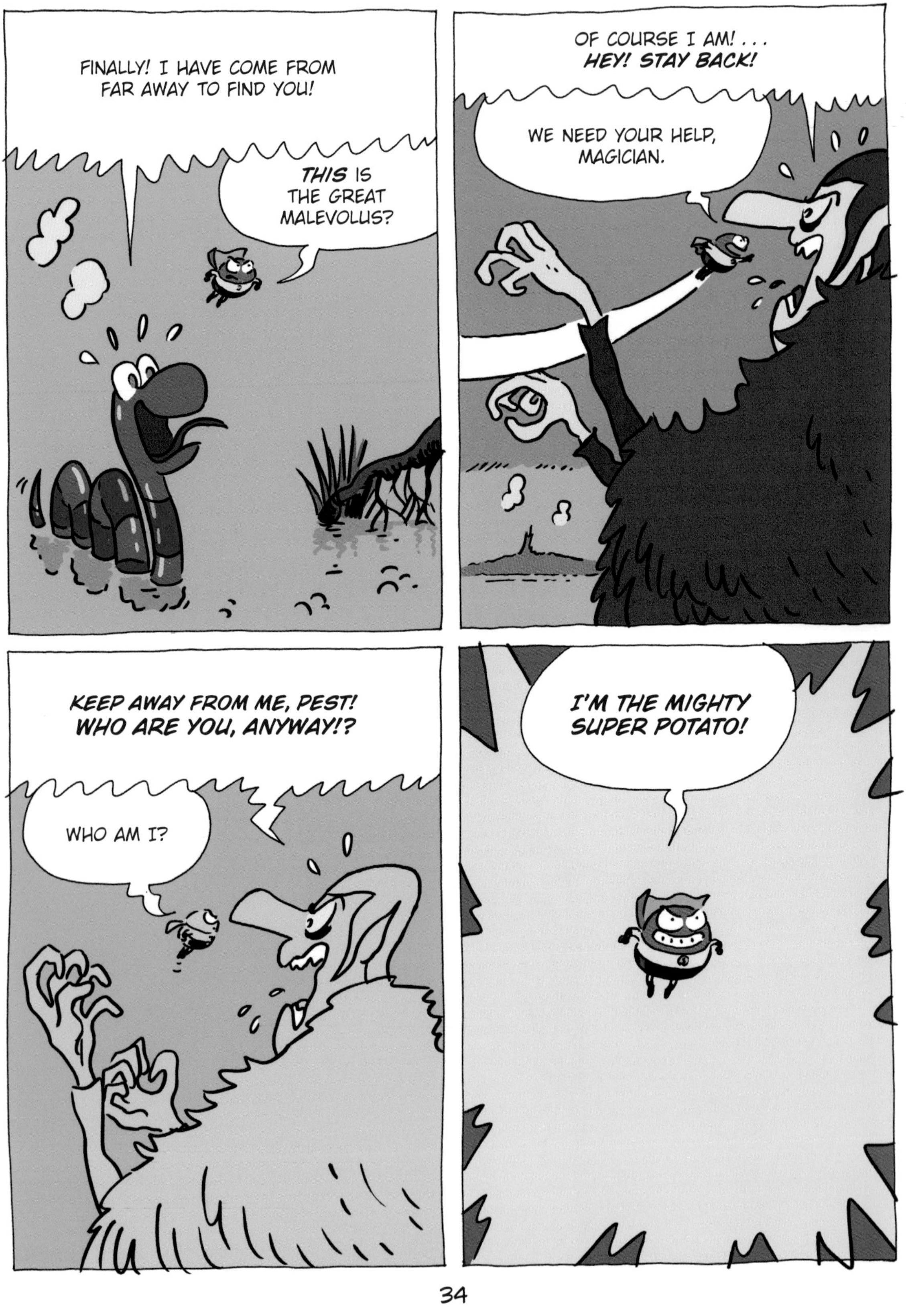
FINALLY! I HAVE COME FROM FAR AWAY TO FIND YOU!
THIS IS THE GREAT MALEVOLUS?
OF COURSE I AM! . . . HEY! STAY BACK!
WE NEED YOUR HELP, MAGICIAN.
KEEP AWAY FROM ME, PEST! WHO ARE YOU, ANYWAY!?
WHO AM I?
I'M THE MIGHTY SUPER POTATO!

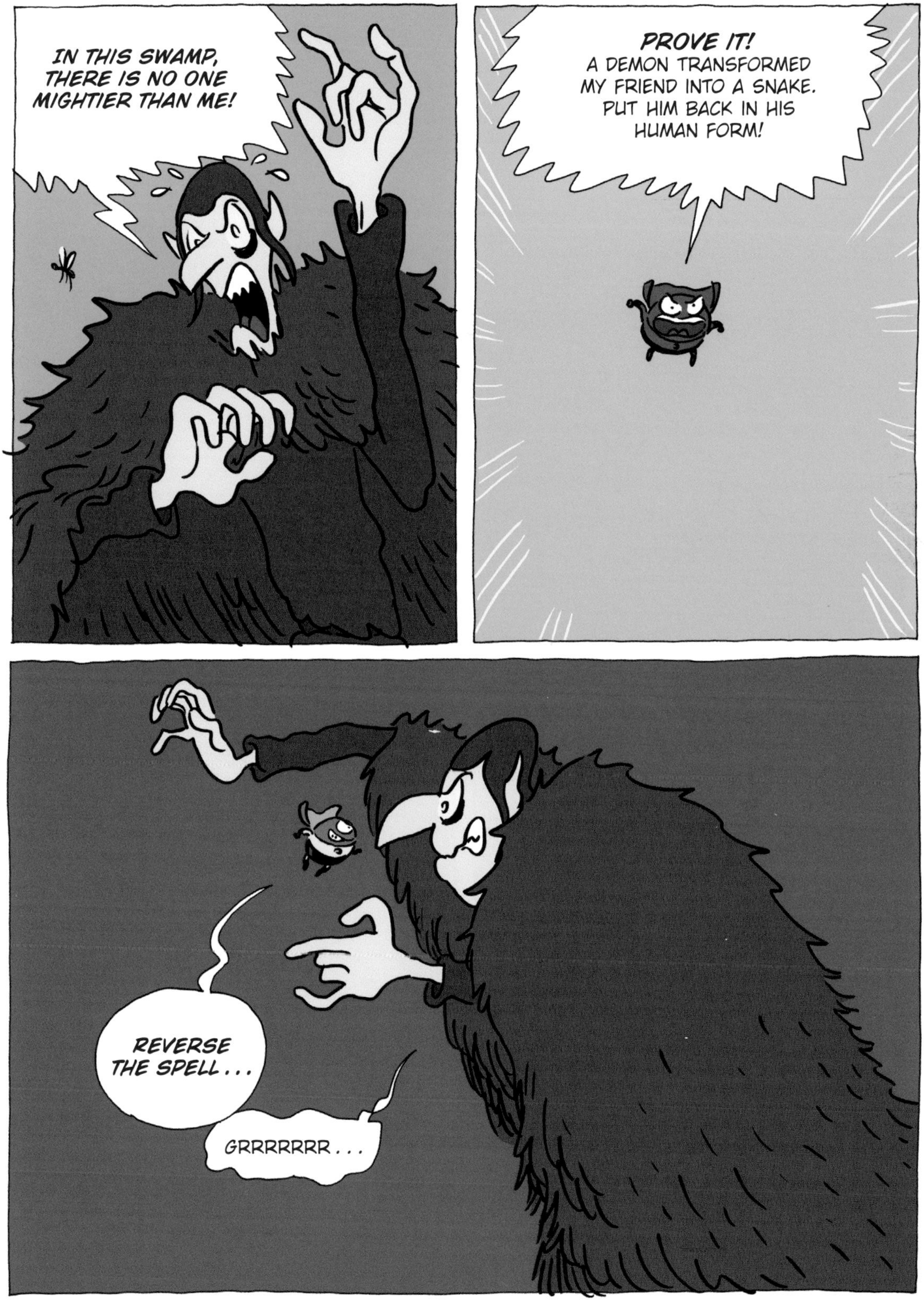
IN THIS SWAMP, THERE IS NO ONE MIGHTIER THAN ME!
PROVE IT! A DEMON TRANSFORMED MY FRIEND INTO A SNAKE. PUT HIM BACK IN HIS HUMAN FORM!
REVERSE THE SPELL . . .
GRRRRRRR . . .

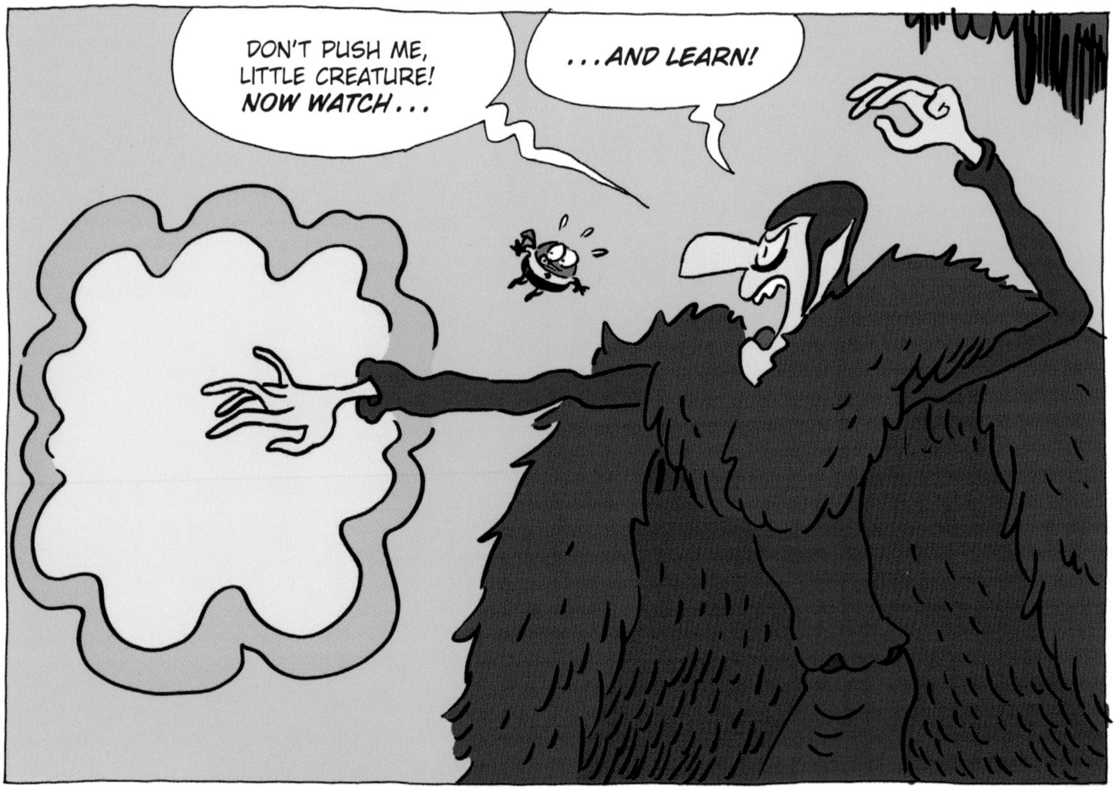
DON'T PUSH ME, LITTLE CREATURE! NOW WATCH . . .
. . . AND LEARN!

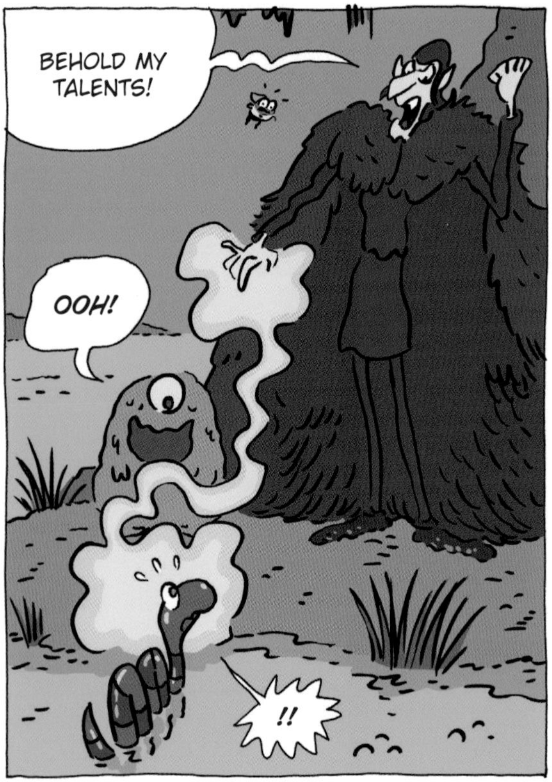
BEHOLD MY TALENTS!
OOH!
!!

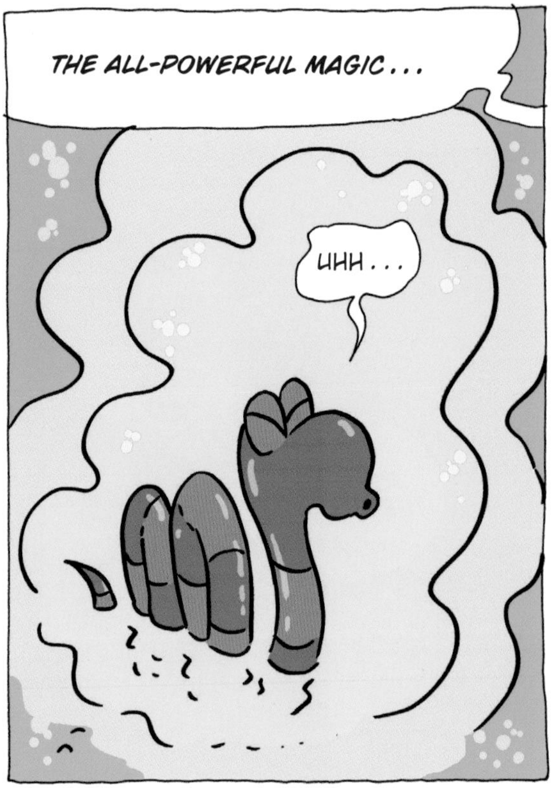
THE ALL-POWERFUL MAGIC . . .
UHH . . .

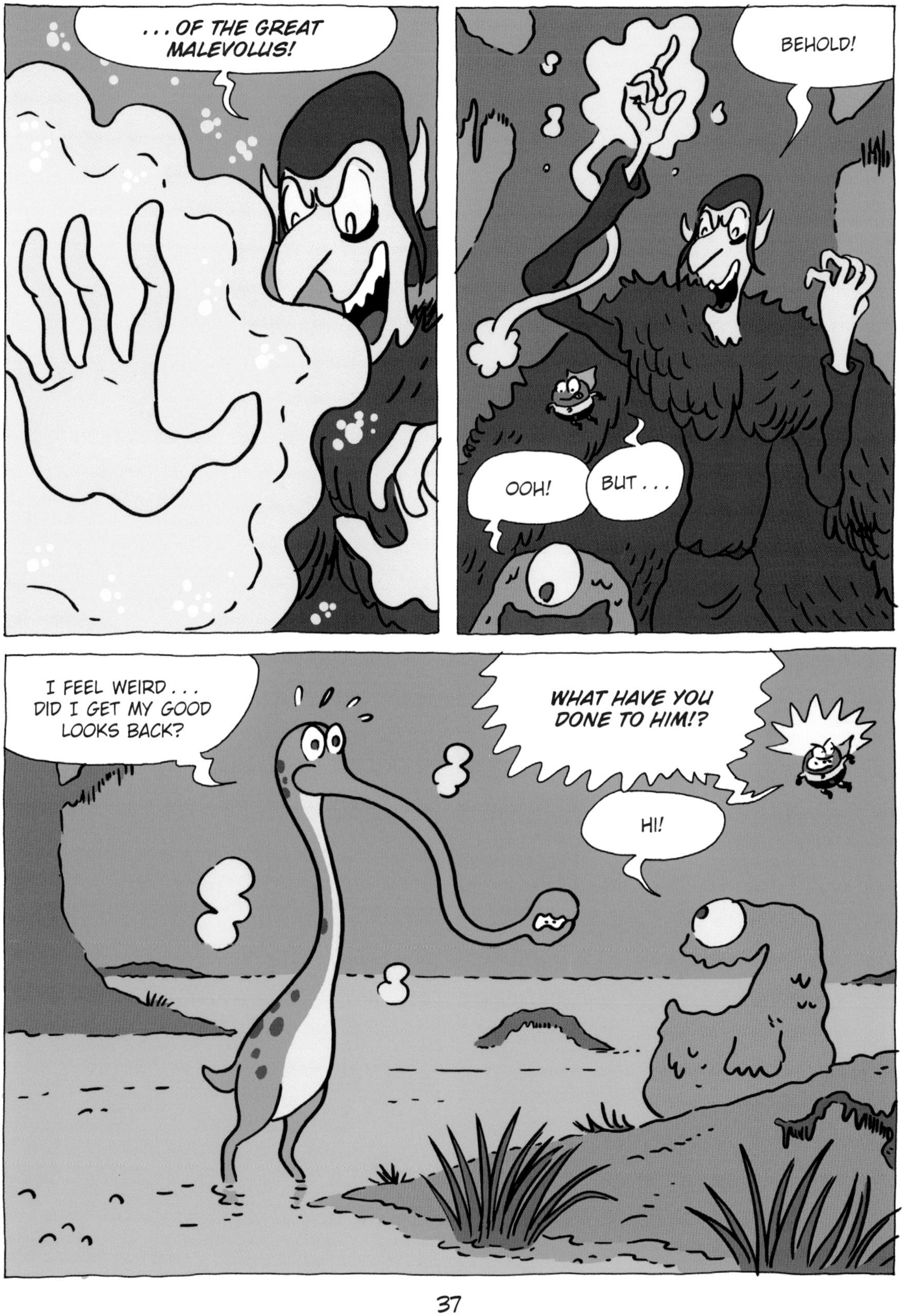
. . . OF THE GREAT MALEVOLUS!
BEHOLD!
OOH!
BUT . . .
I FEEL WEIRD . . . DID I GET MY GOOD LOOKS BACK?
WHAT HAVE YOU DONE TO HIM!?
HI!

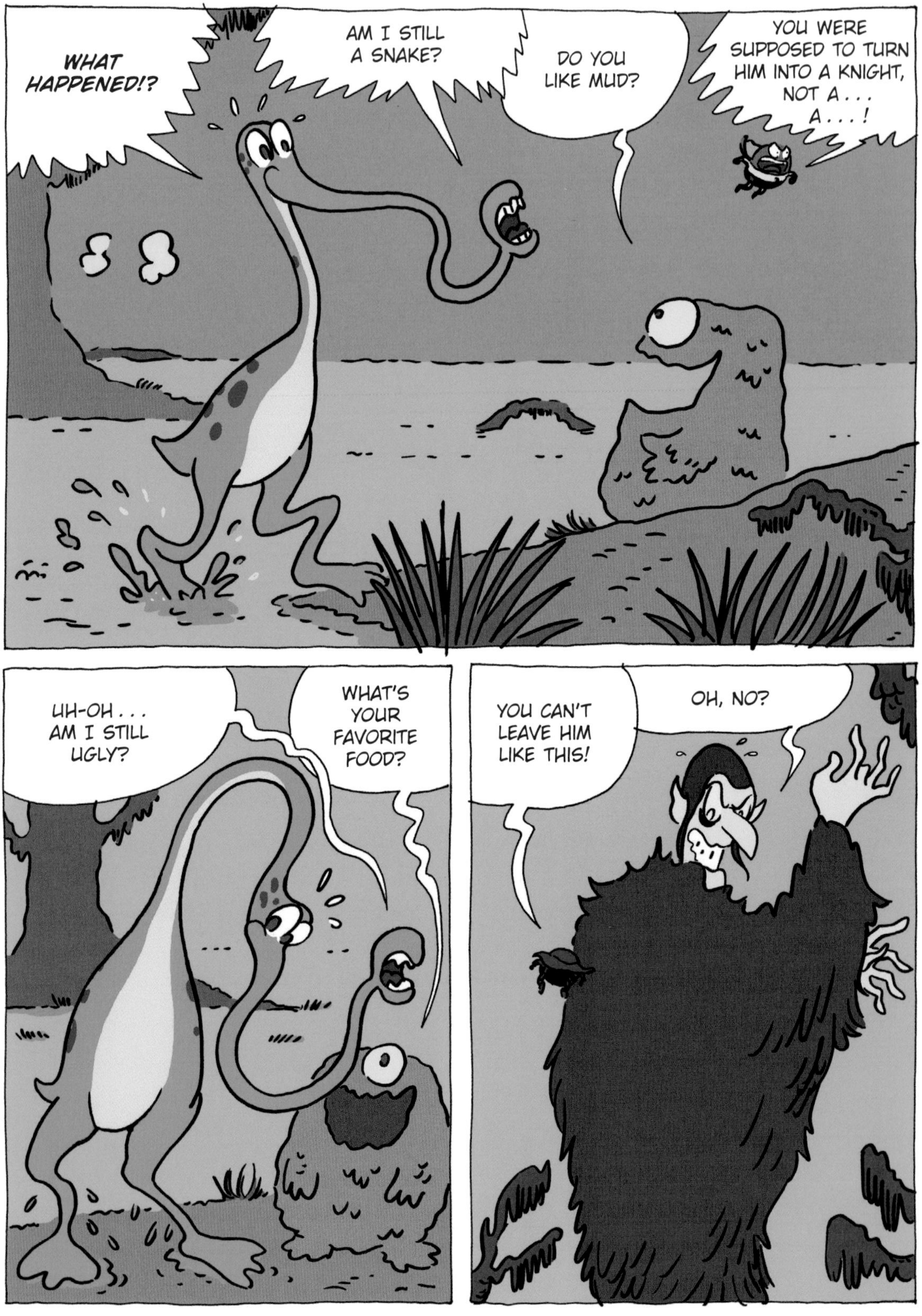
WHAT HAPPENED!?
AM I STILL A SNAKE?
DO YOU LIKE MUD?
YOU WERE SUPPOSED TO TURN HIM INTO A KNIGHT, NOT A . . . A . . . !
UH-OH . . . AM I STILL UGLY?
WHAT'S YOUR FAVORITE FOOD?
YOU CAN'T LEAVE HIM LIKE THIS!
OH, NO?

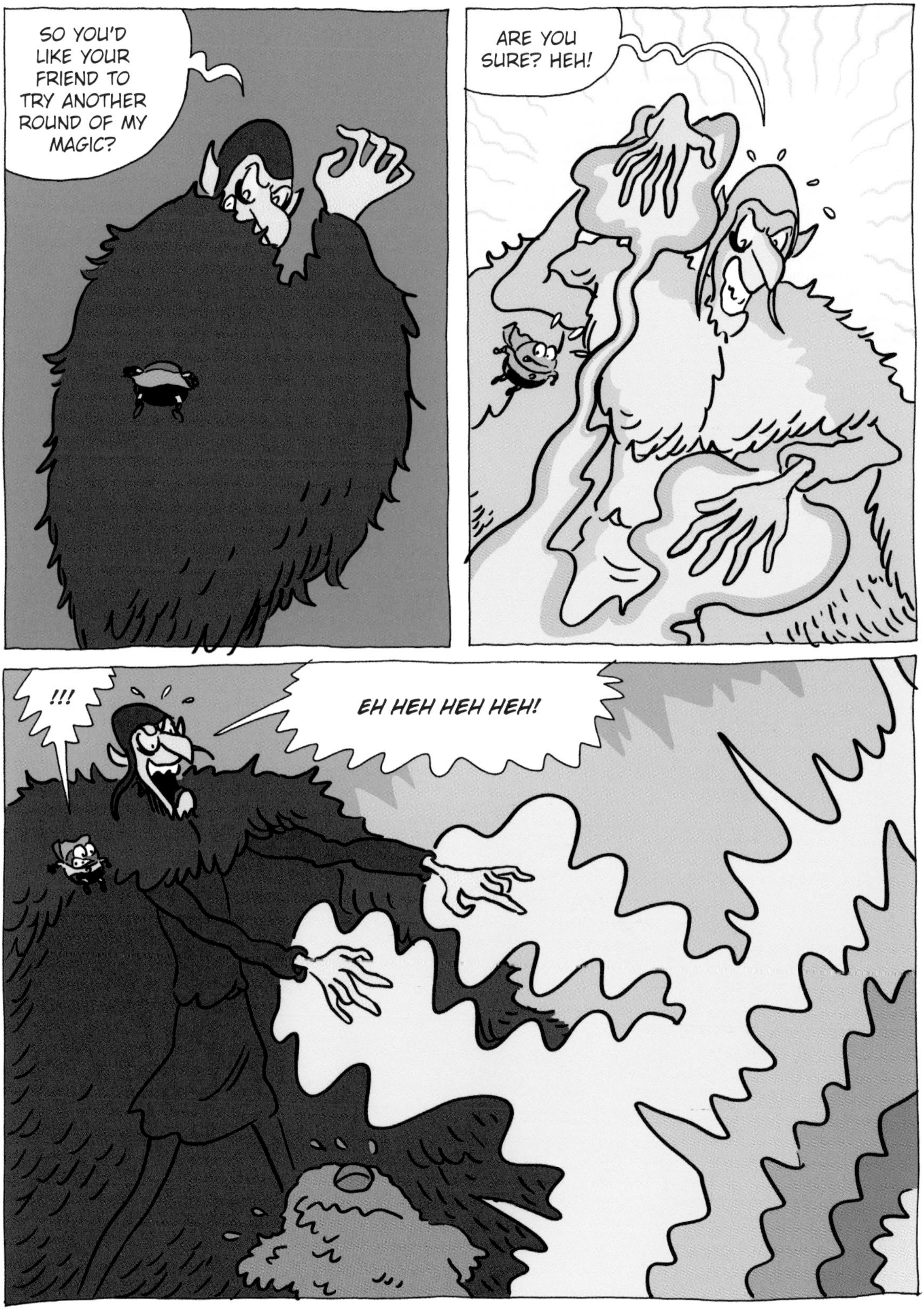
SO YOU'D LIKE YOUR FRIEND TO TRY ANOTHER ROUND OF MY MAGIC?
ARE YOU SURE? HEH!
!!!
EH HEH HEH HEH!

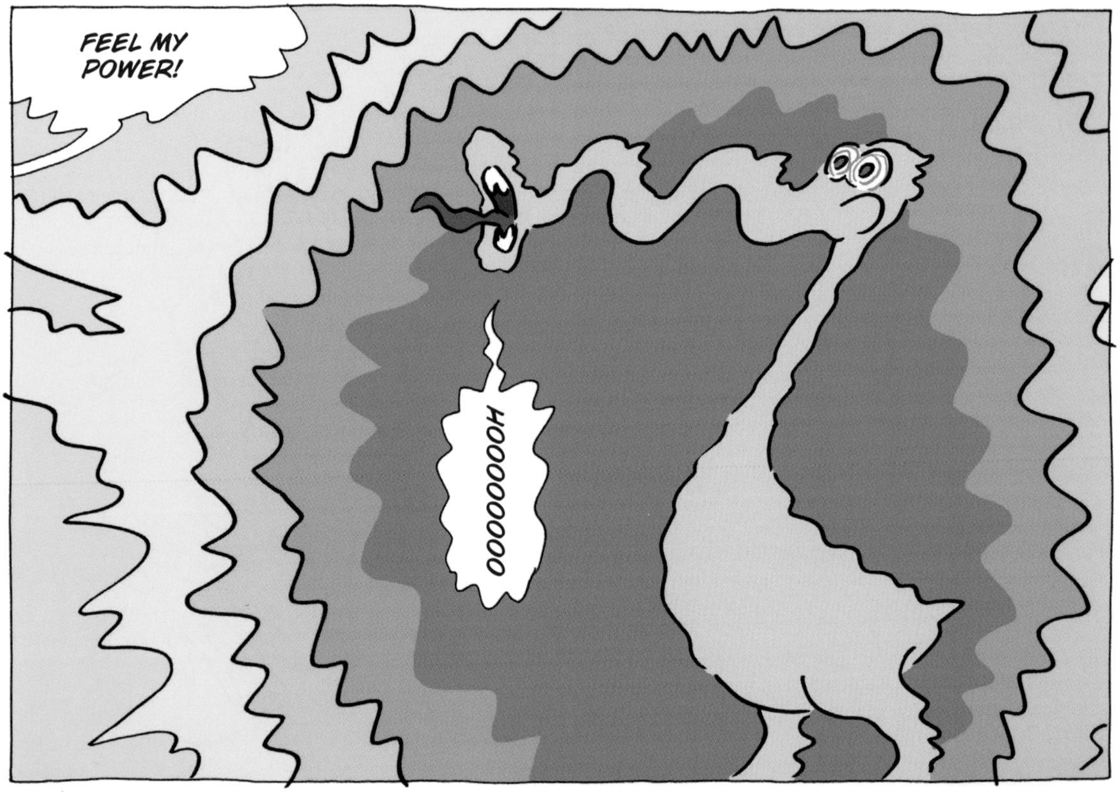
FEEL MY POWER!
HOOOOOOOOO

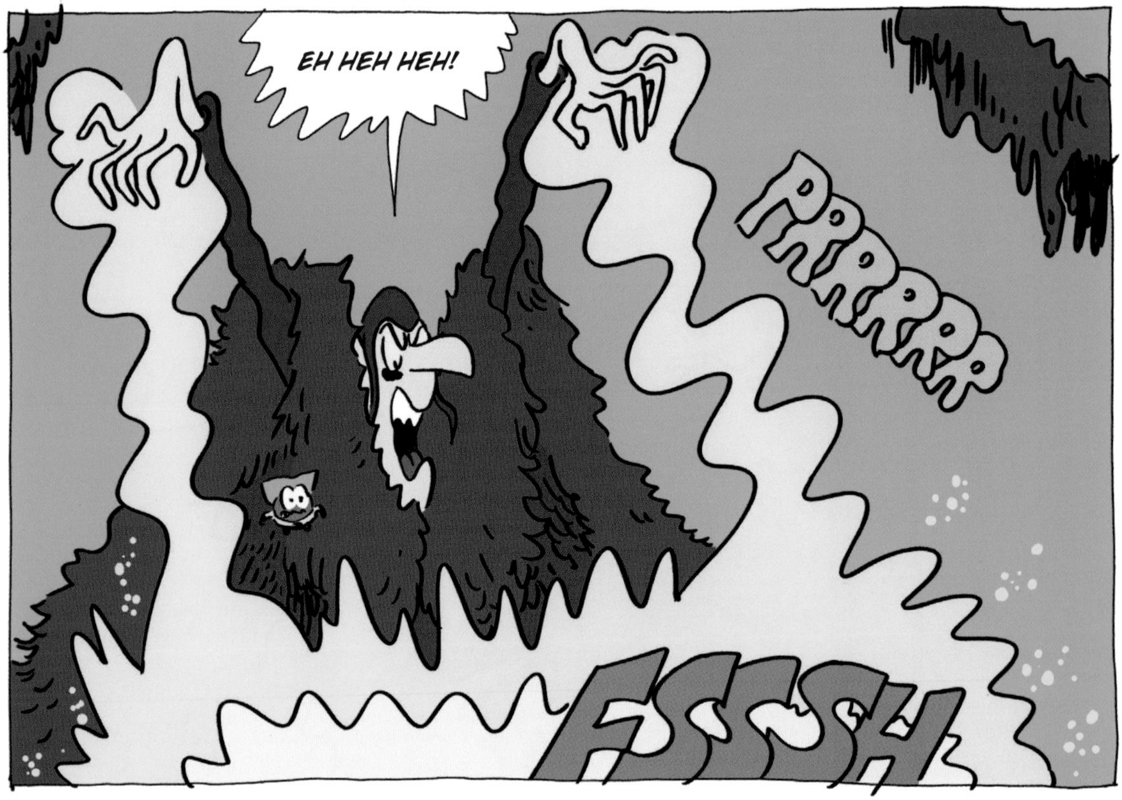
EH HEH HEH!
PRRRRRR
FSSSH

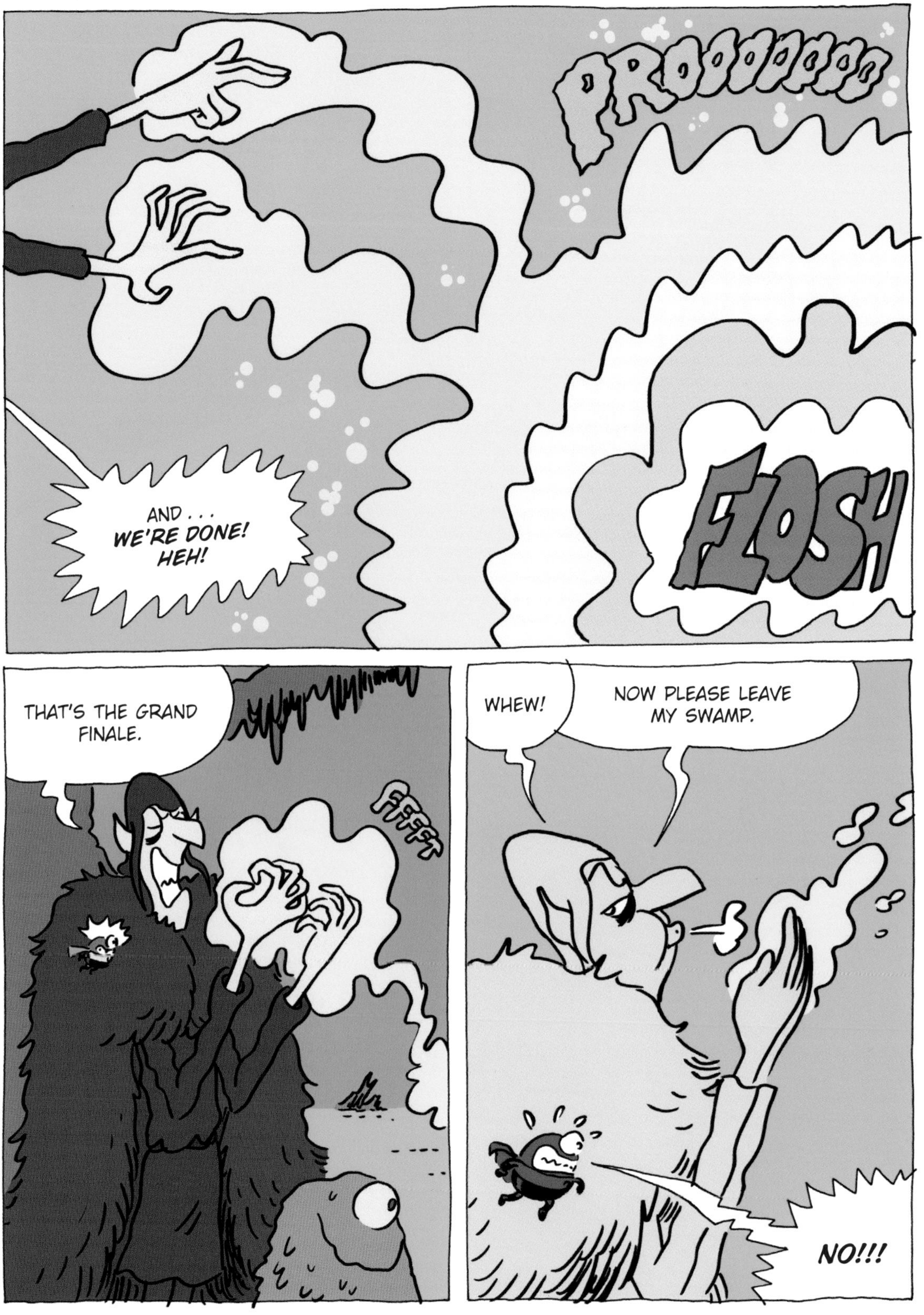
PROOOOOOO
AND . . . WE'RE DONE! HEH!
FLOSH
THAT'S THE GRAND FINALE.
FFFFT
WHEW!
NOW PLEASE LEAVE MY SWAMP.
NO!!!

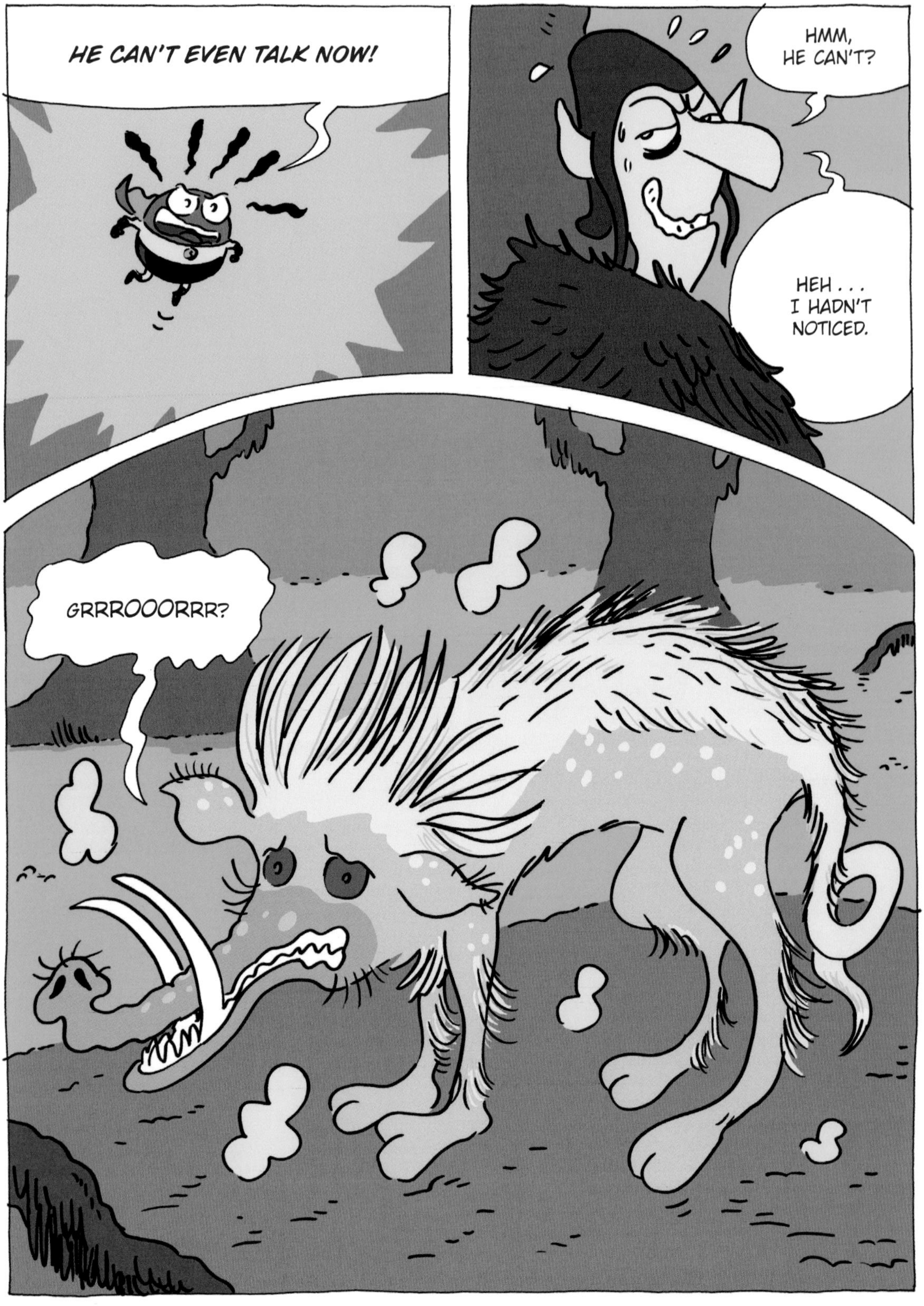
HE CAN'T EVEN TALK NOW!
HMM, HE CAN'T?
HEH . . . I HADN'T NOTICED.
GRRROOORRR?

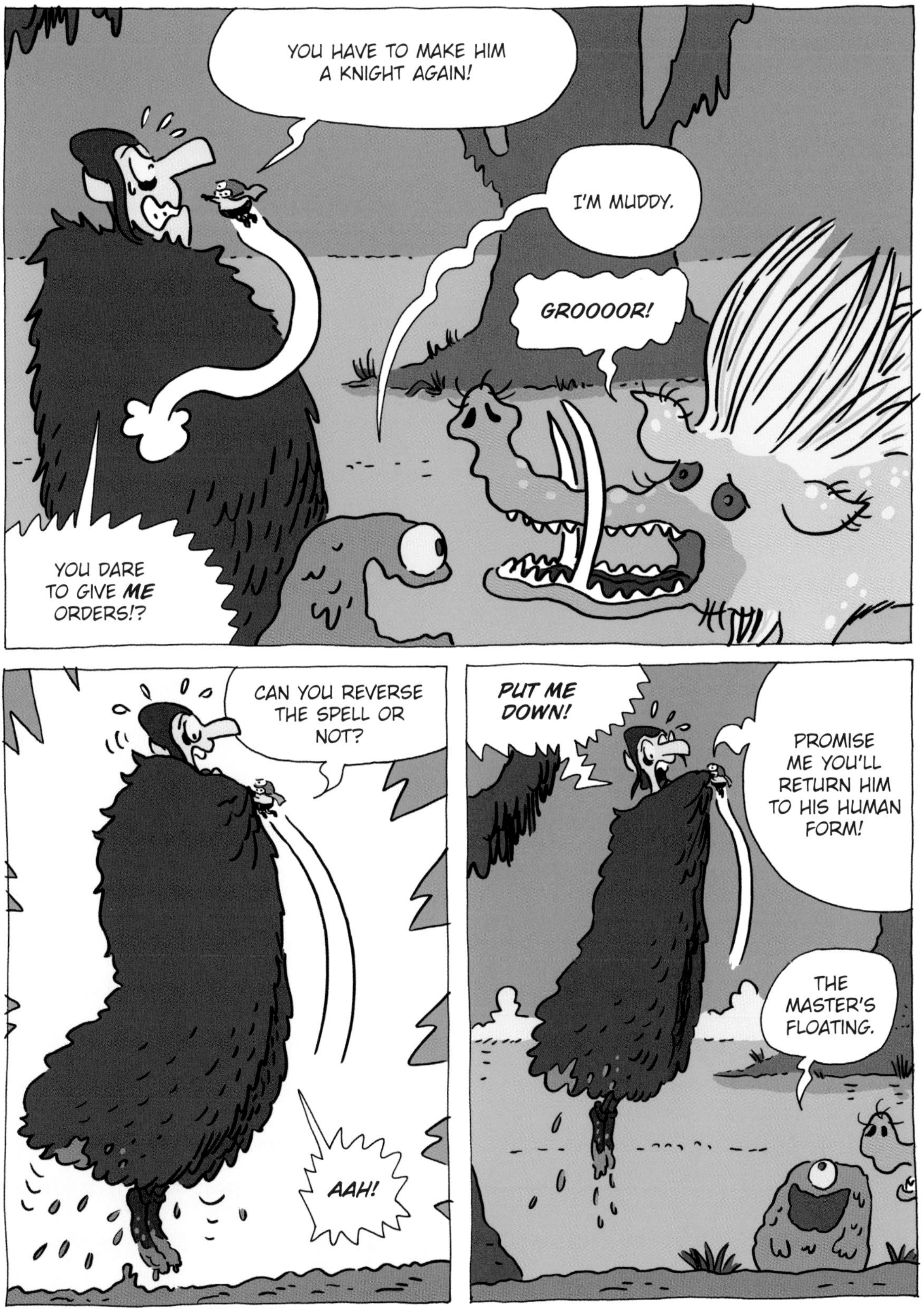
YOU HAVE TO MAKE HIM A KNIGHT AGAIN!
YOU DARE TO GIVE ME ORDERS!?
I'M MUDDY.
GROOOOR!
CAN YOU REVERSE THE SPELL OR NOT?
AAH!
PUT ME DOWN!
PROMISE ME YOU'LL RETURN HIM TO HIS HUMAN FORM!
THE MASTER'S FLOATING.

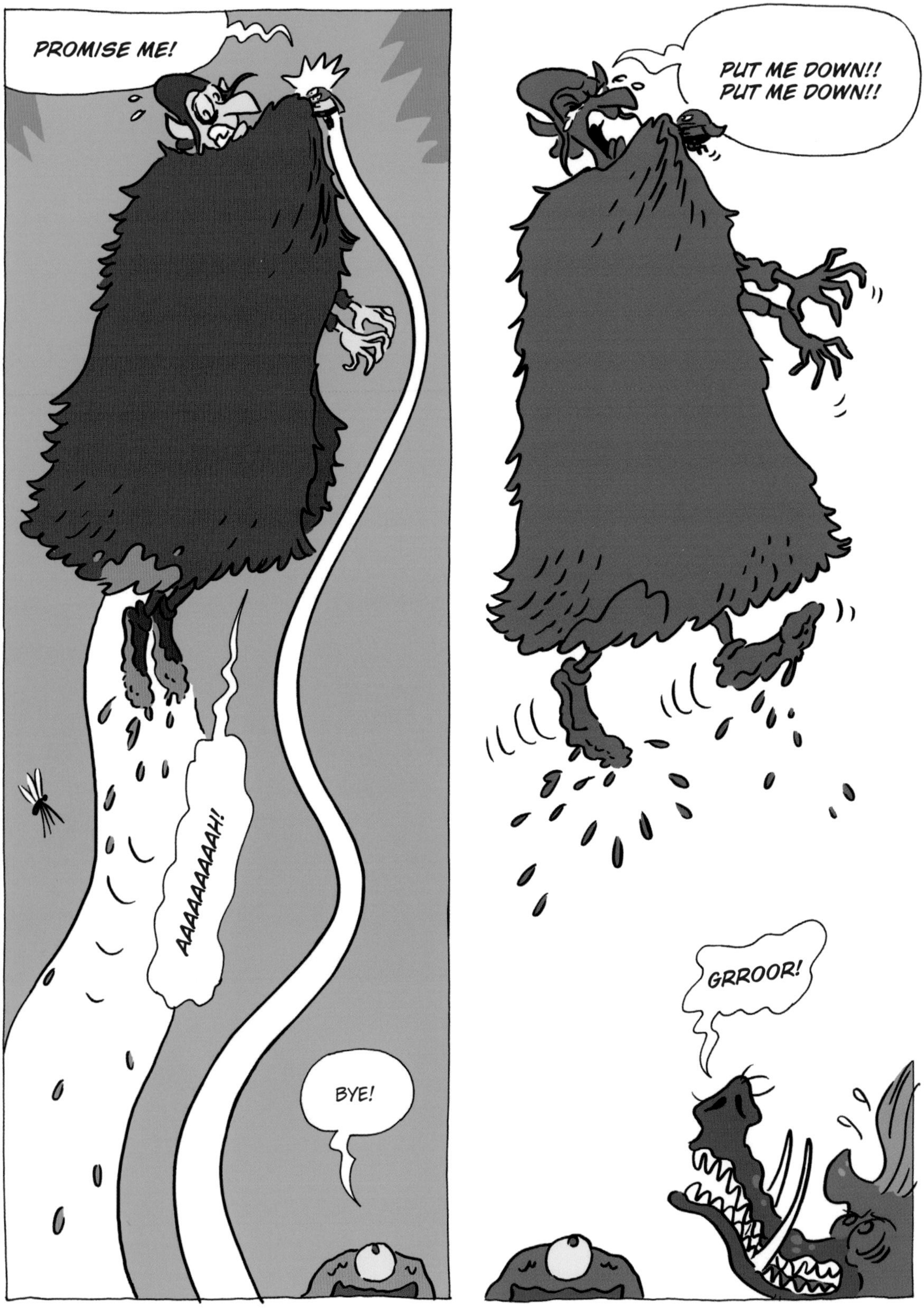
PROMISE ME!
AAAAAAAAAAH!
BYE!
PUT ME DOWN!!
PUT ME DOWN!!
GRROOR!

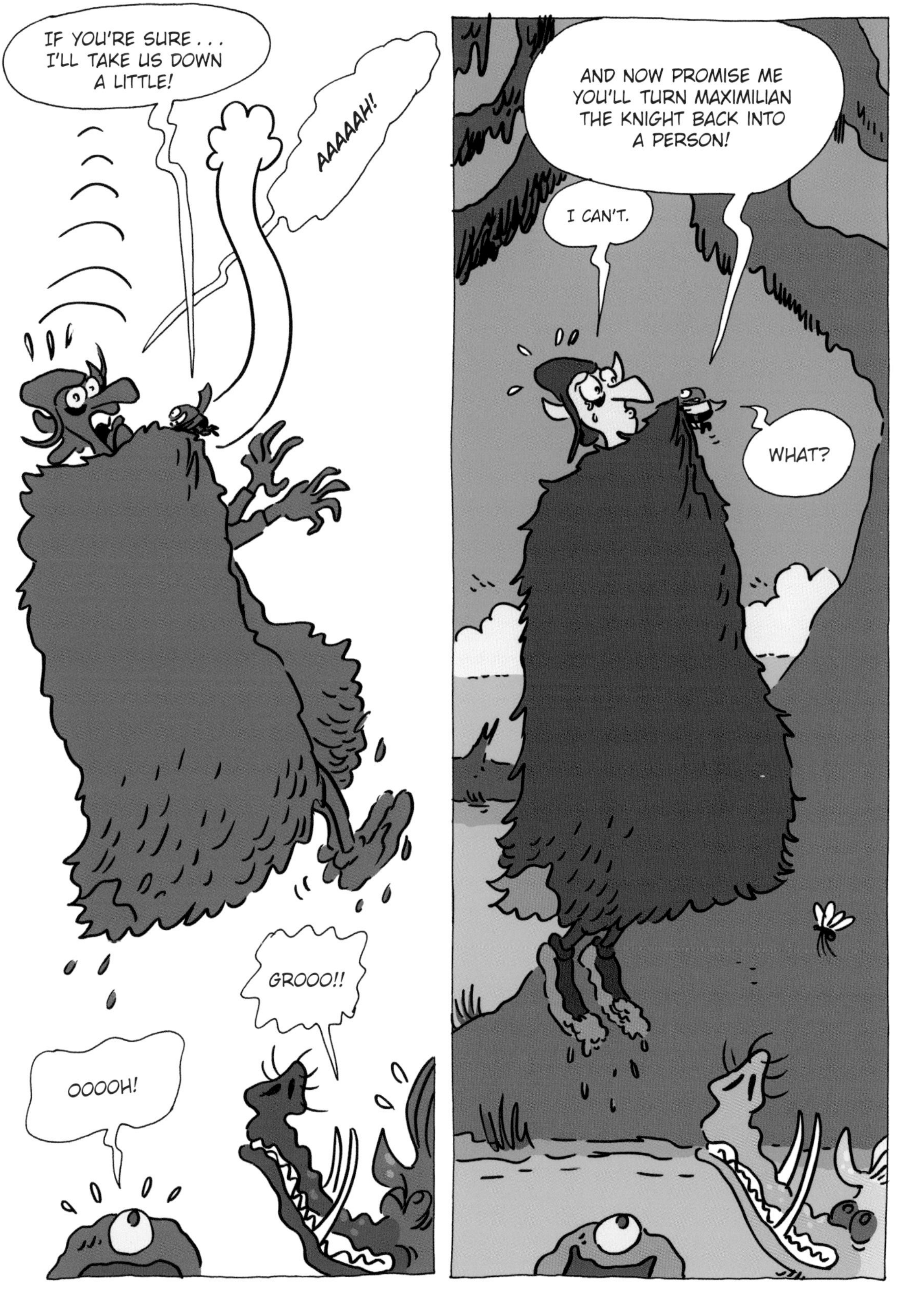

IF YOU'RE SURE . . . I'LL TAKE US DOWN A LITTLE!
AAAAAH!
GROOO!!
OOOOH!
AND NOW PROMISE ME YOU'LL TURN MAXIMILIAN THE KNIGHT BACK INTO A PERSON!
I CAN'T.
WHAT?

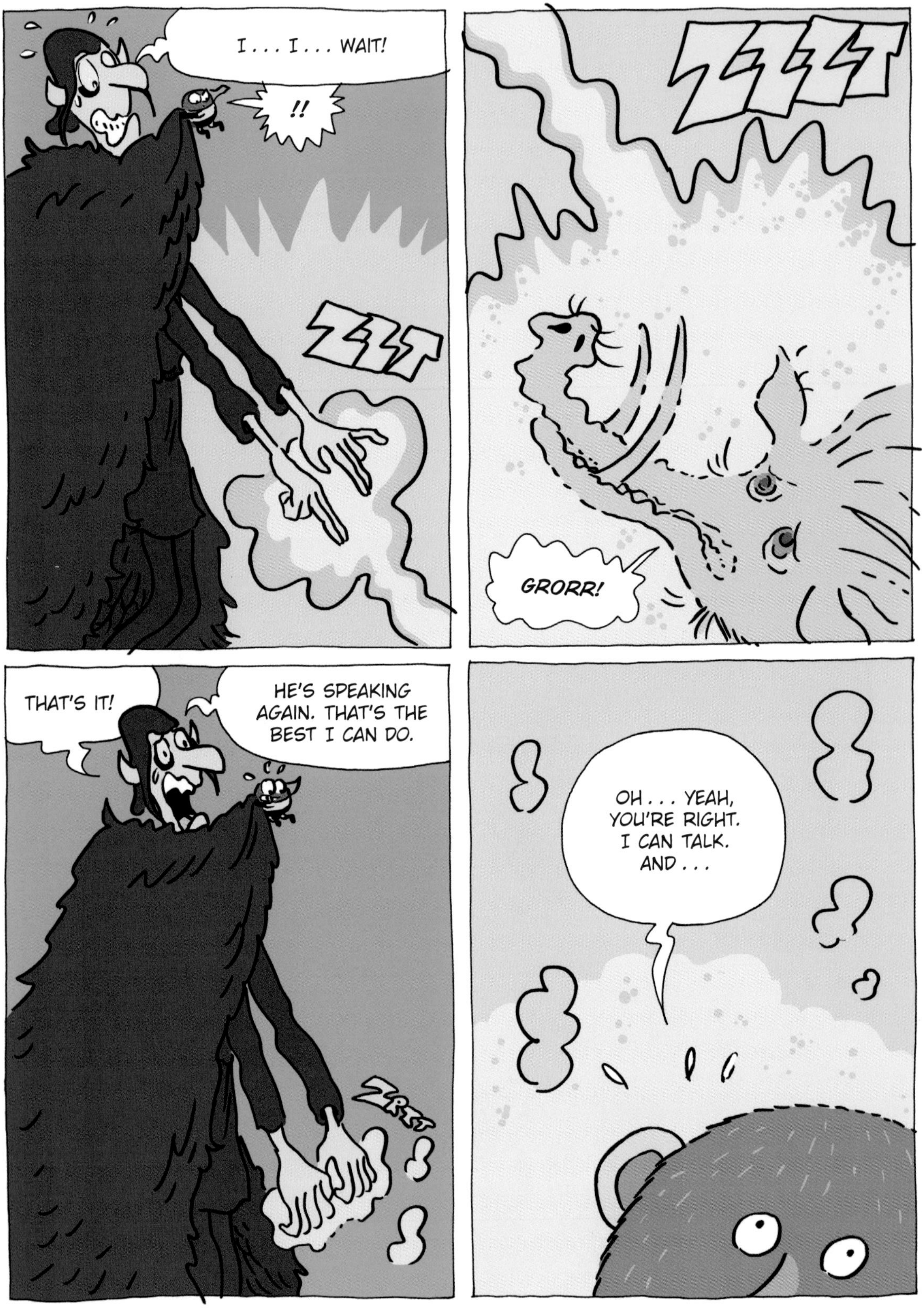
I . . . I . . . WAIT!
!!
ZZZT
ZZZT
GRORR!
THAT'S IT!
HE'S SPEAKING AGAIN. THAT'S THE BEST I CAN DO.
OH . . . YEAH, YOU'RE RIGHT. I CAN TALK. AND . . .

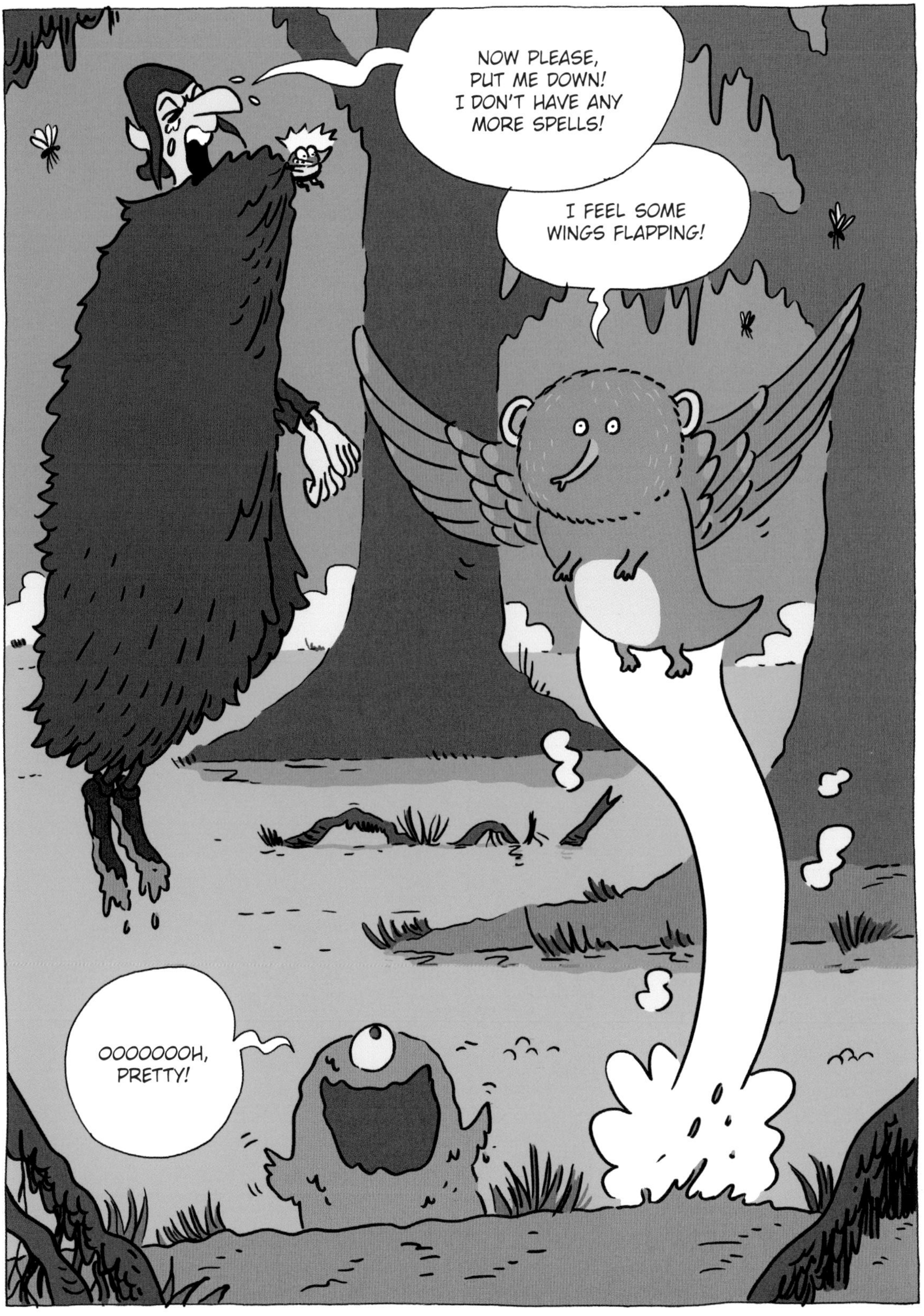
NOW PLEASE, PUT ME DOWN! I DON'T HAVE ANY MORE SPELLS!
I FEEL SOME WINGS FLAPPING!
OOOOOOOH, PRETTY!

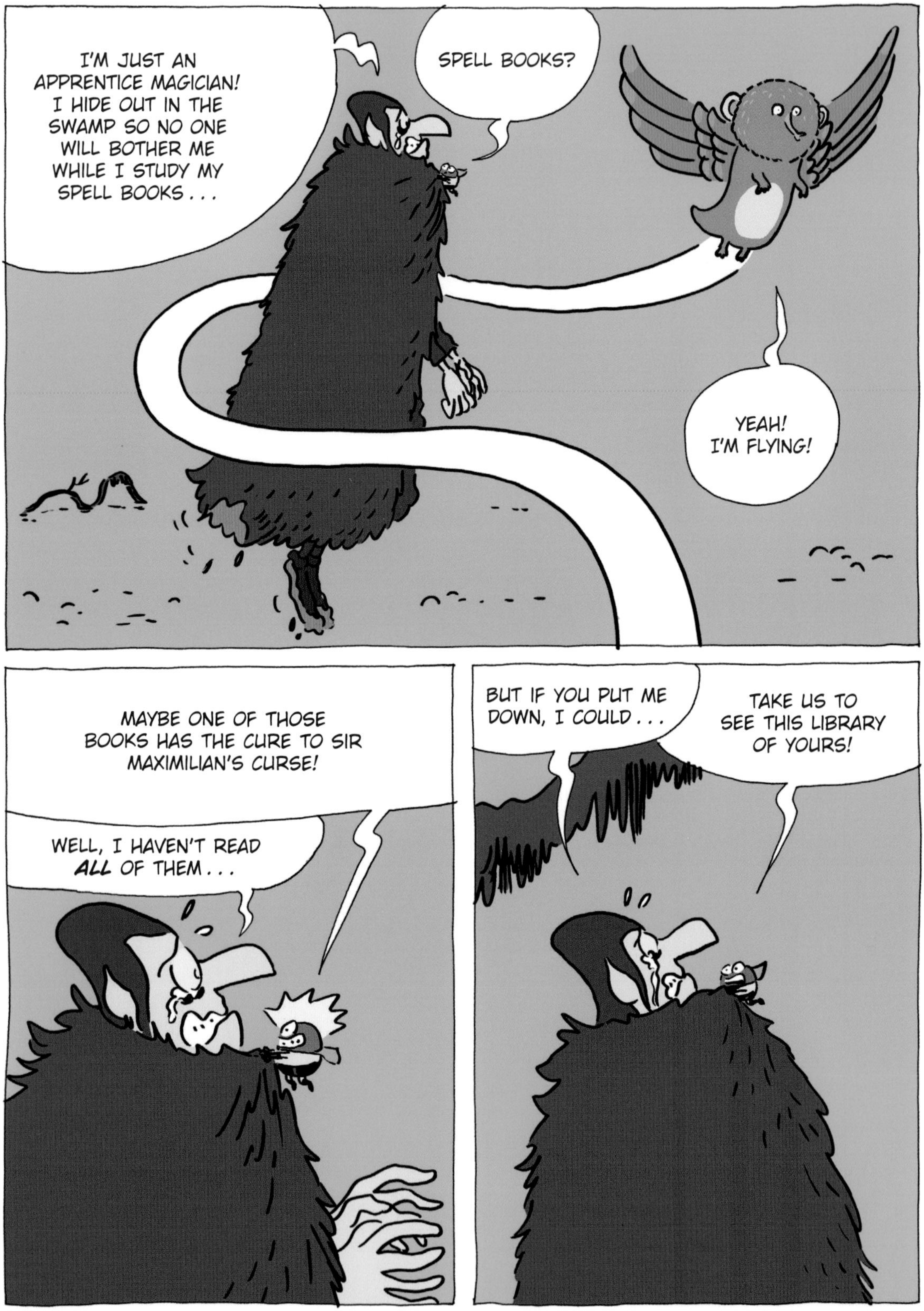
I'M JUST AN APPRENTICE MAGICIAN! I HIDE OUT IN THE SWAMP SO NO ONE WILL BOTHER ME WHILE I STUDY MY SPELL BOOKS . . .
SPELL BOOKS?
YEAH! I'M FLYING!
MAYBE ONE OF THOSE BOOKS HAS THE CURE TO SIR MAXIMILIAN'S CURSE!
WELL, I HAVEN'T READ ***ALL*** OF THEM . . .
BUT IF YOU PUT ME DOWN, I COULD . . .
TAKE US TO SEE THIS LIBRARY OF YOURS!

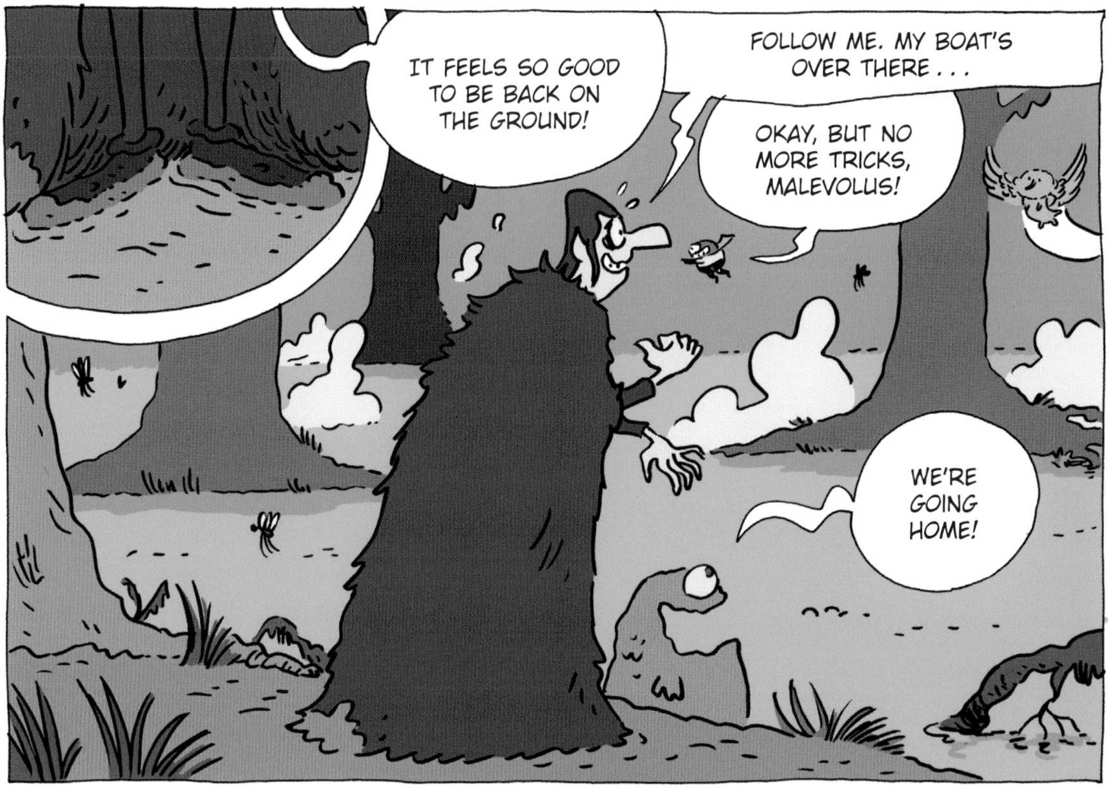
IT FEELS SO GOOD TO BE BACK ON THE GROUND!
FOLLOW ME. MY BOAT'S OVER THERE . . .
OKAY, BUT NO MORE TRICKS, MALEVOLUS!
WE'RE GOING HOME!

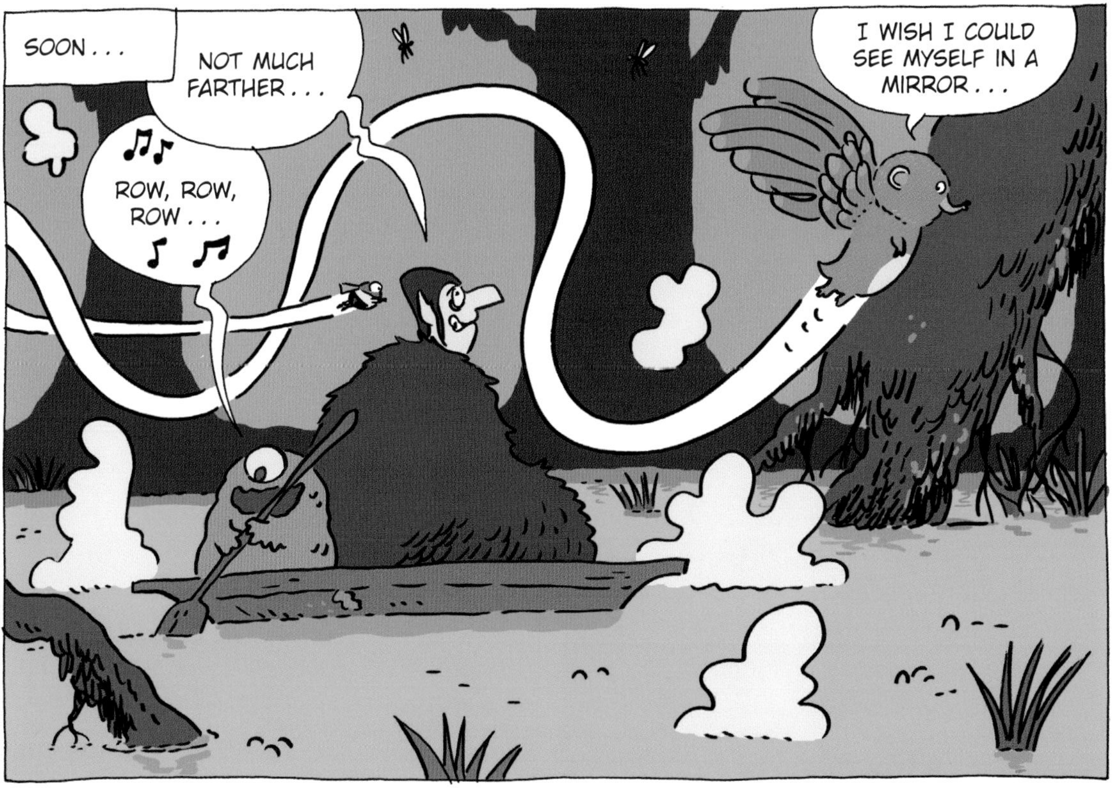
SOON . . .
NOT MUCH FARTHER . . .
ROW, ROW, ROW . . .
I WISH I COULD SEE MYSELF IN A MIRROR . . .

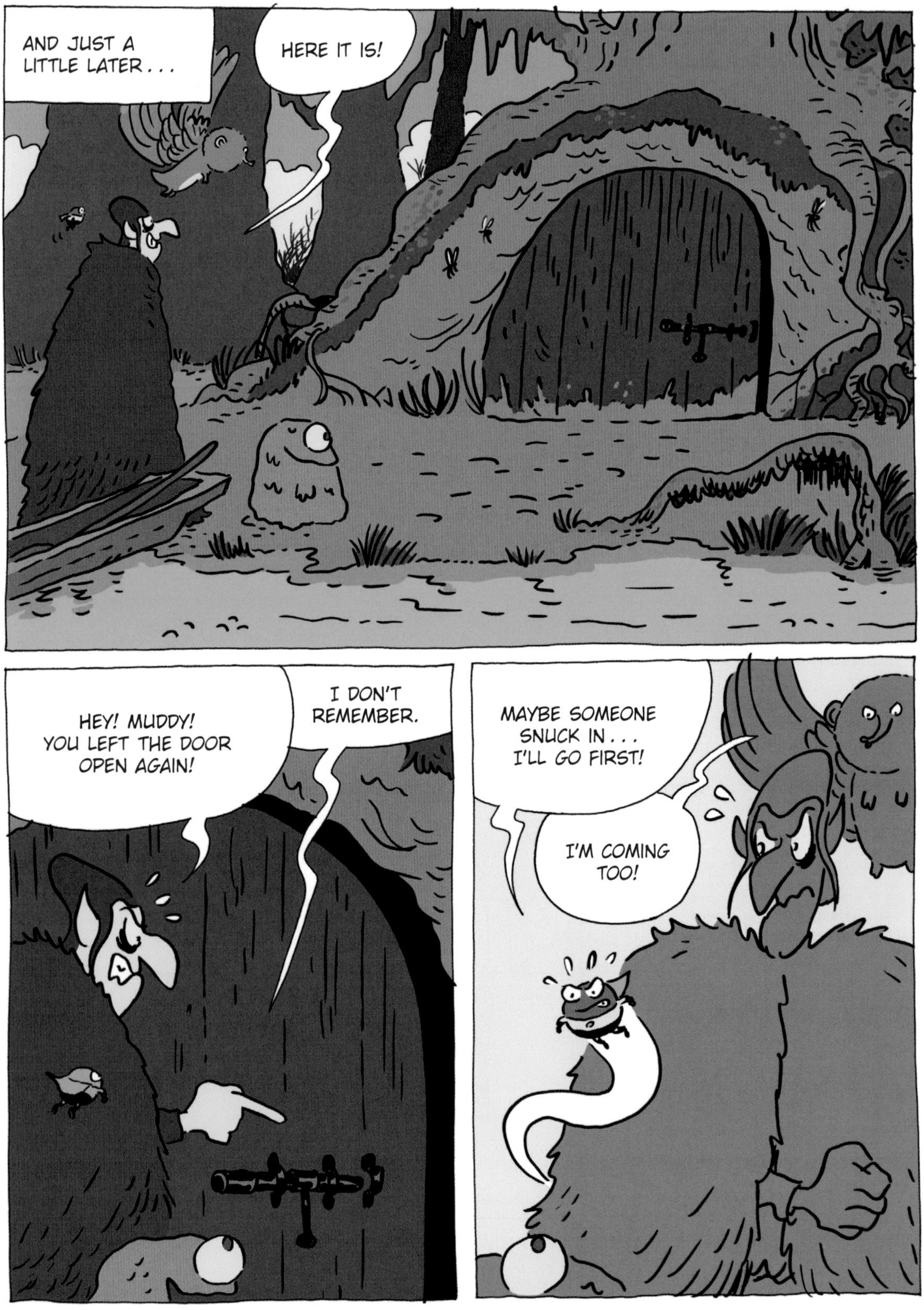
AND JUST A LITTLE LATER . . .
HERE IT IS!
HEY! MUDDY! YOU LEFT THE DOOR OPEN AGAIN!
I DON'T REMEMBER.
MAYBE SOMEONE SNUCK IN . . . I'LL GO FIRST!
I'M COMING TOO!

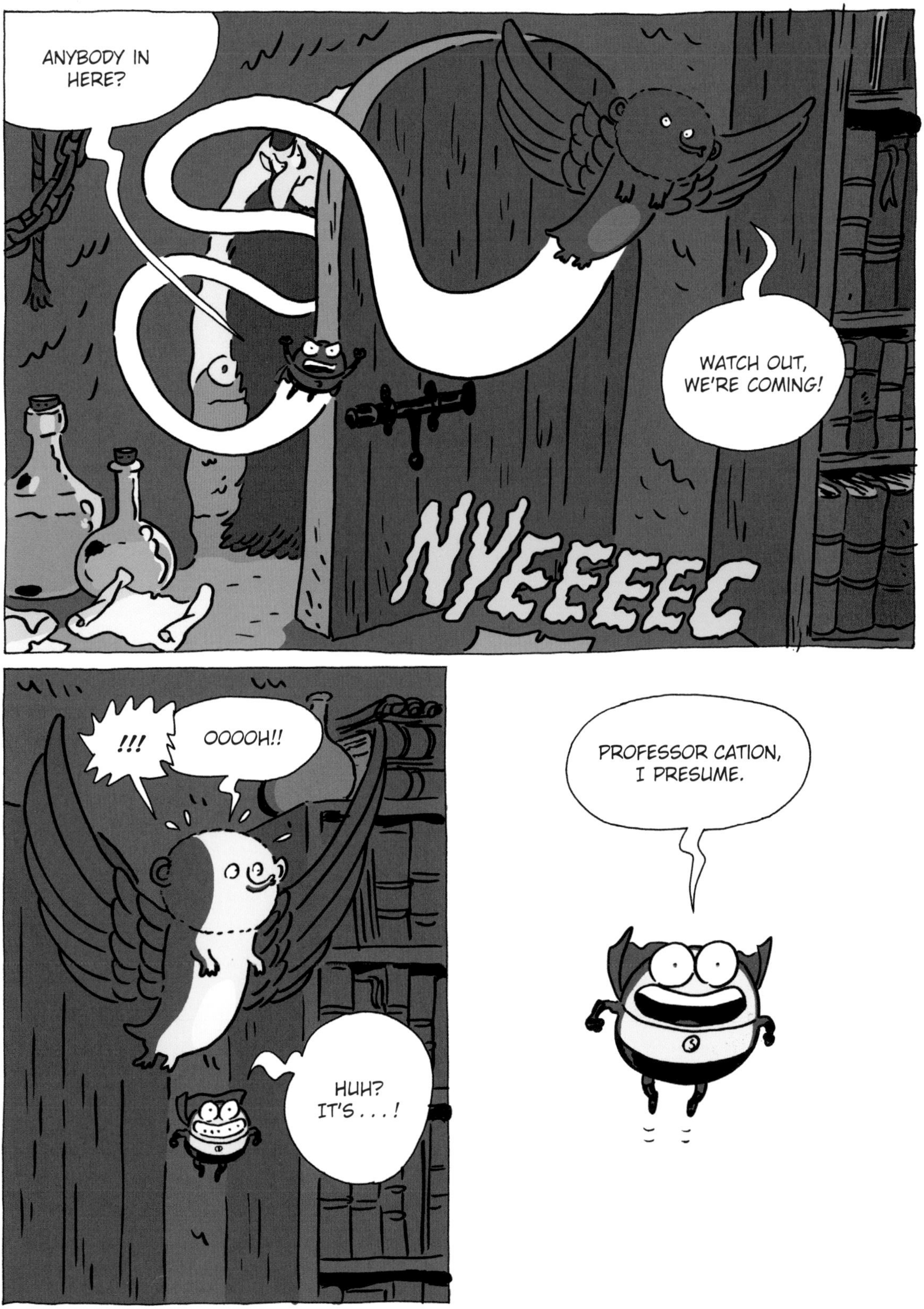
ANYBODY IN HERE?
WATCH OUT, WE'RE COMING!
NYEEEEC
!!!
OOOOH!!
HUH? IT'S . . . !
PROFESSOR CATION, I PRESUME.

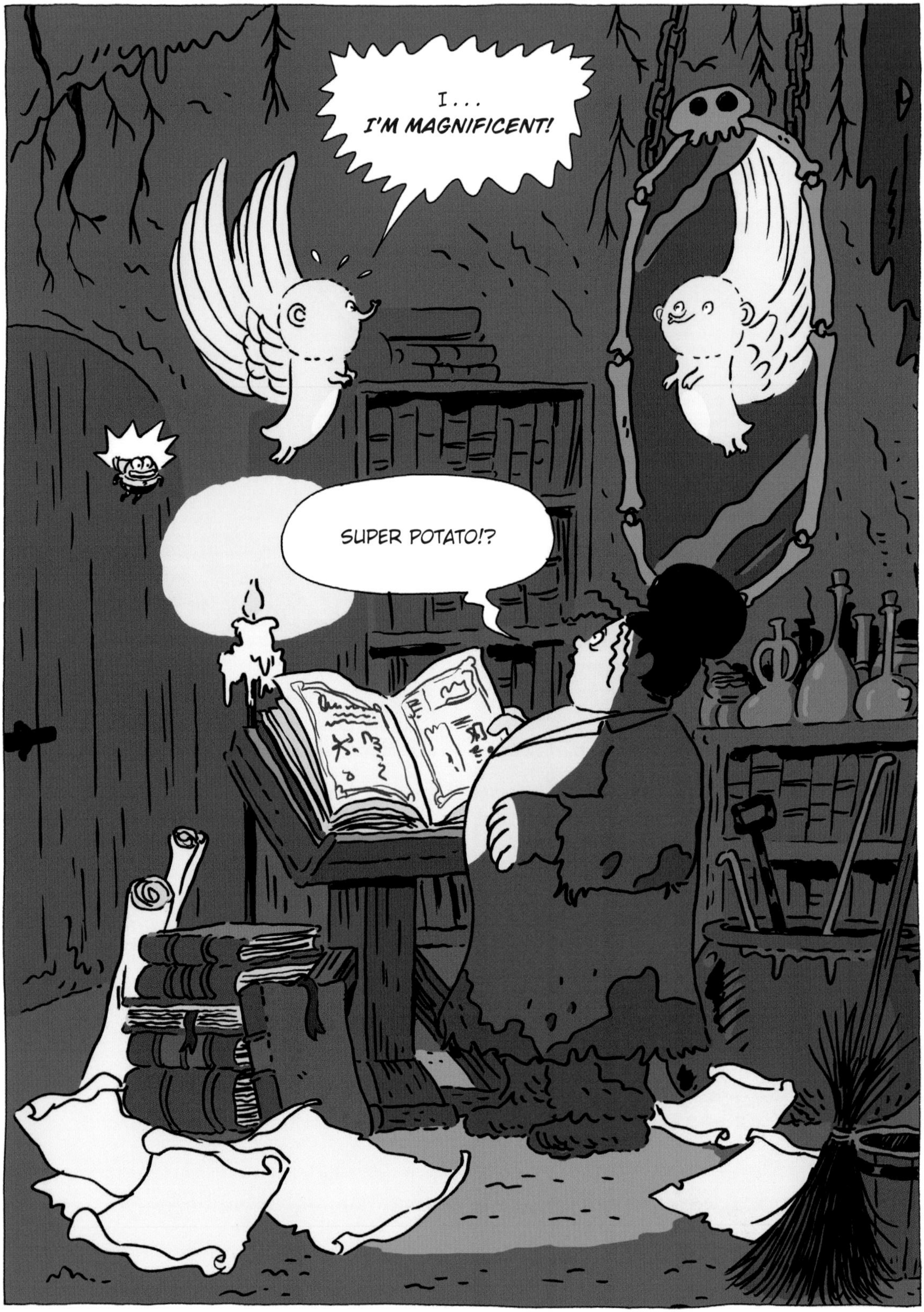
I . . .
I'M MAGNIFICENT!
SUPER POTATO!?

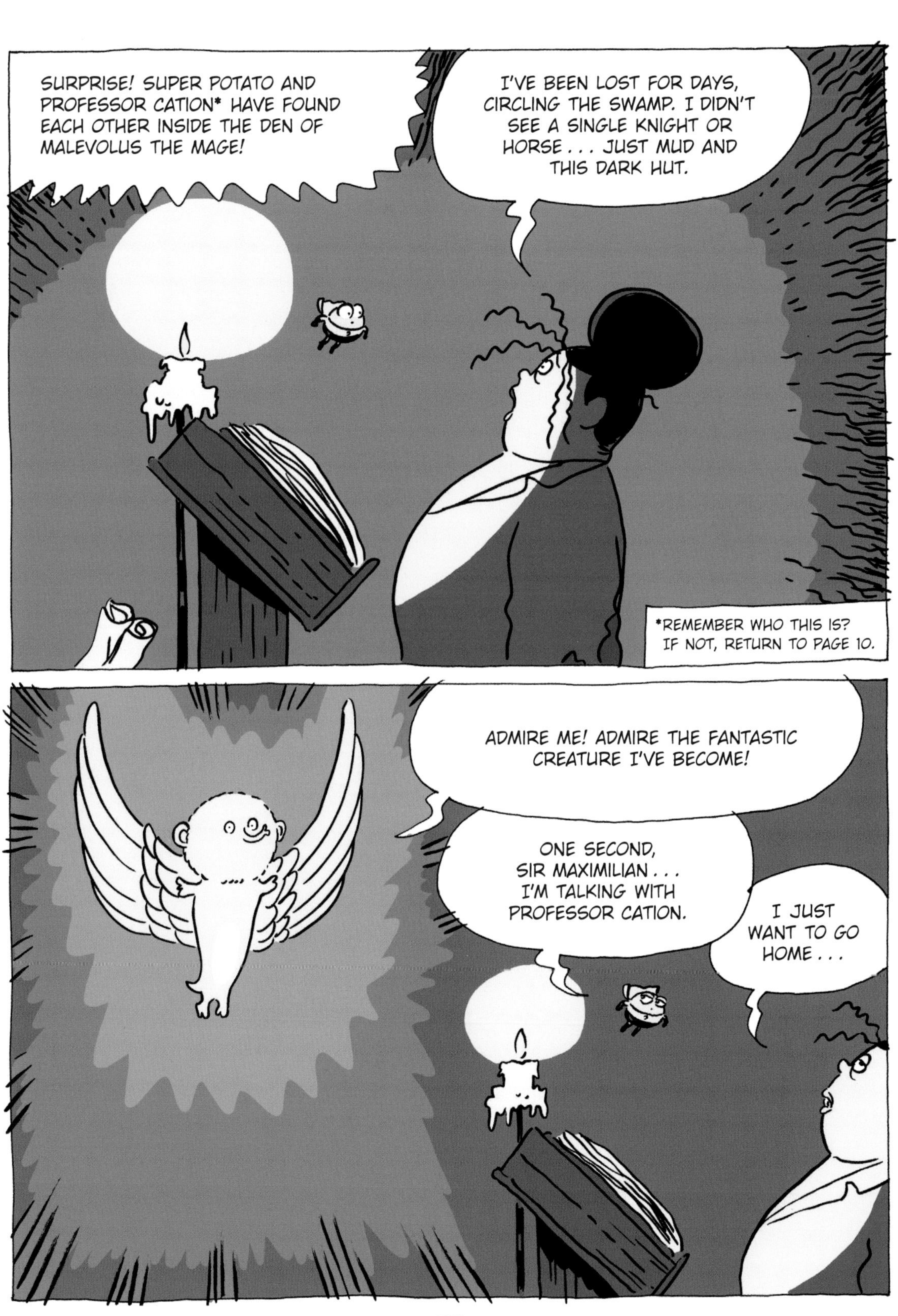
SURPRISE! SUPER POTATO AND PROFESSOR CATION* HAVE FOUND EACH OTHER INSIDE THE DEN OF MALEVOLUS THE MAGE!
I'VE BEEN LOST FOR DAYS, CIRCLING THE SWAMP. I DIDN'T SEE A SINGLE KNIGHT OR HORSE . . . JUST MUD AND THIS DARK HUT.
*REMEMBER WHO THIS IS? IF NOT, RETURN TO PAGE 10.
ADMIRE ME! ADMIRE THE FANTASTIC CREATURE I'VE BECOME!
ONE SECOND, SIR MAXIMILIAN . . . I'M TALKING WITH PROFESSOR CATION.
I JUST WANT TO GO HOME . . .

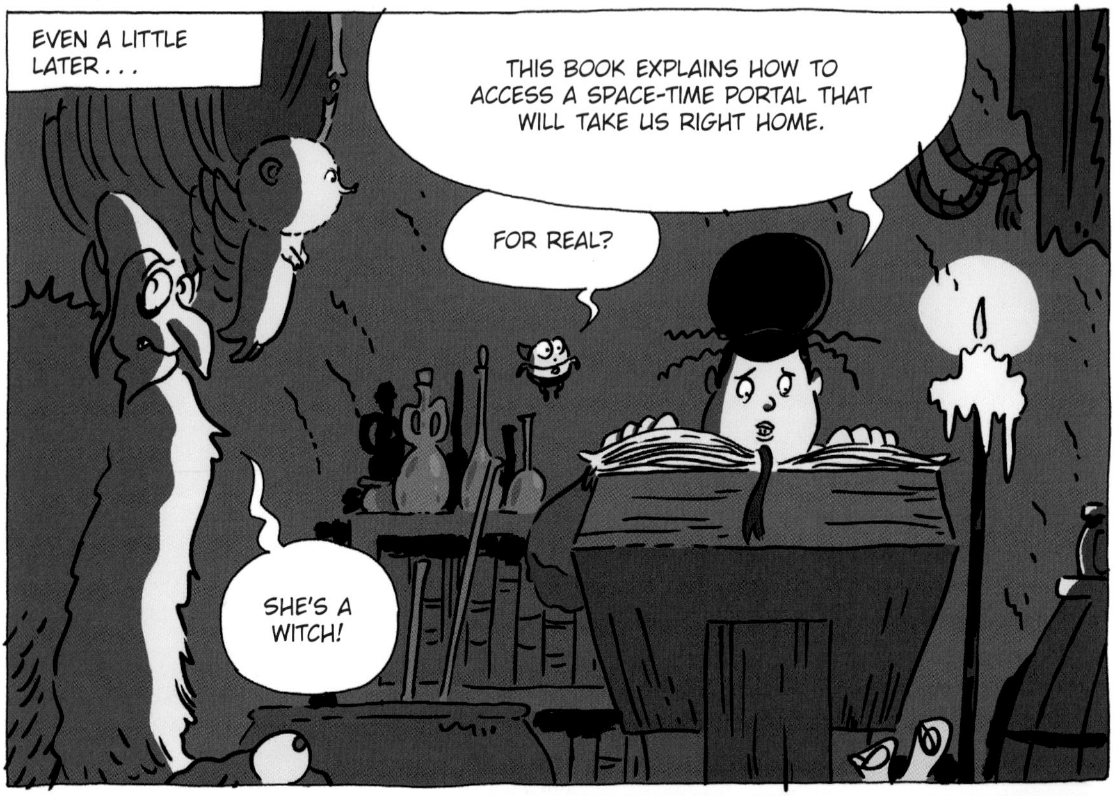
EVEN A LITTLE LATER . . .
THIS BOOK EXPLAINS HOW TO ACCESS A SPACE-TIME PORTAL THAT WILL TAKE US RIGHT HOME.
FOR REAL?
SHE'S A WITCH!

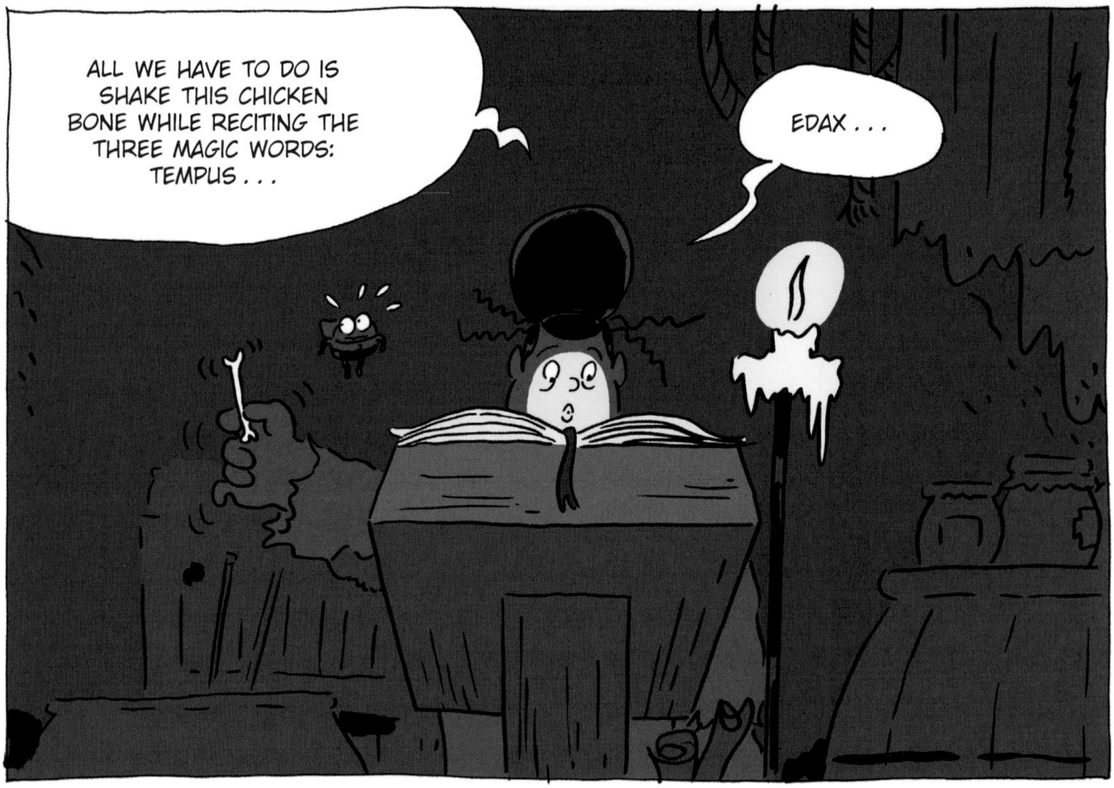
ALL WE HAVE TO DO IS SHAKE THIS CHICKEN BONE WHILE RECITING THE THREE MAGIC WORDS: TEMPUS . . .
EDAX . . .

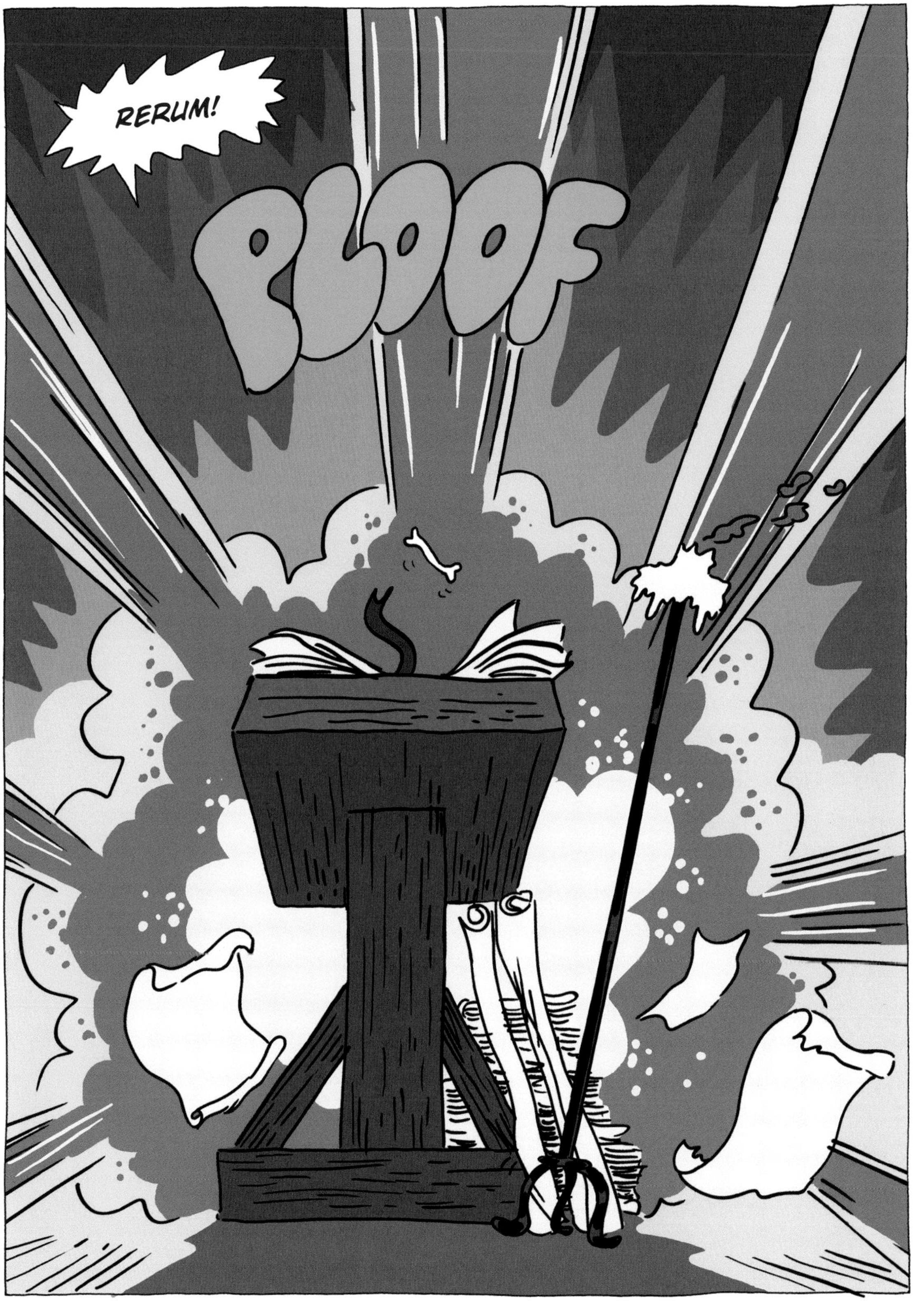
RERUM!
PLOOF

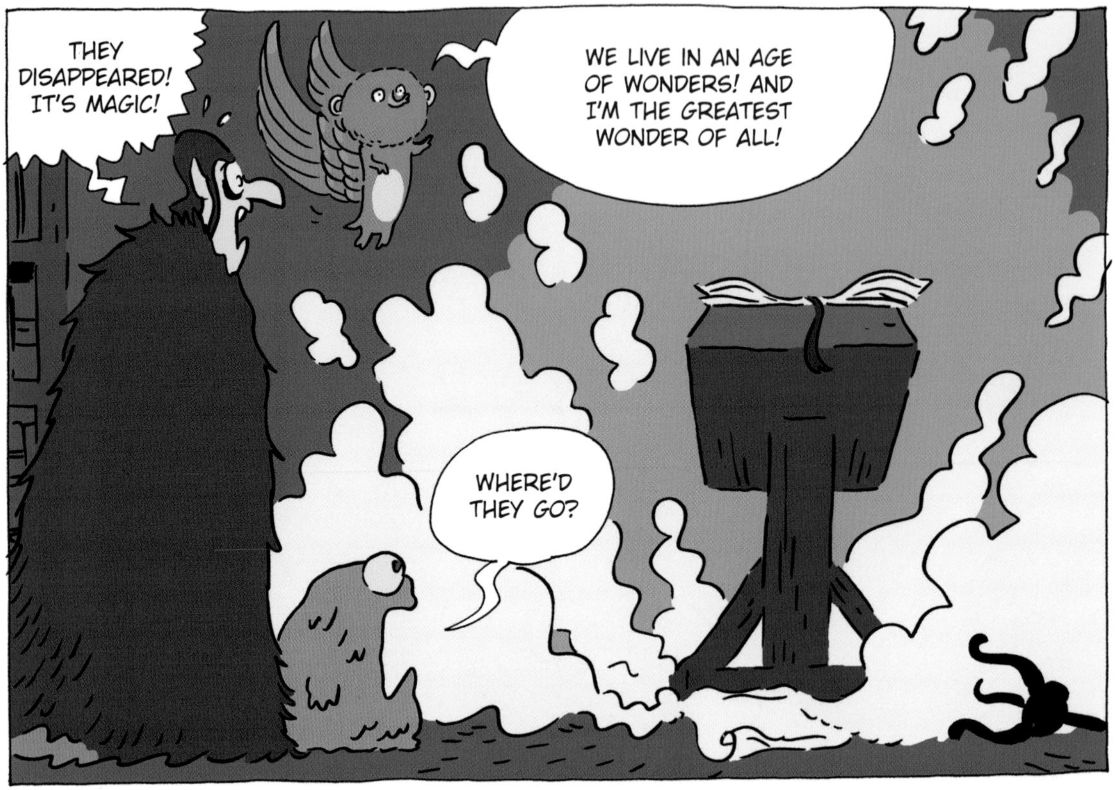
THEY DISAPPEARED! IT'S MAGIC!
WE LIVE IN AN AGE OF WONDERS! AND I'M THE GREATEST WONDER OF ALL!
WHERE'D THEY GO?

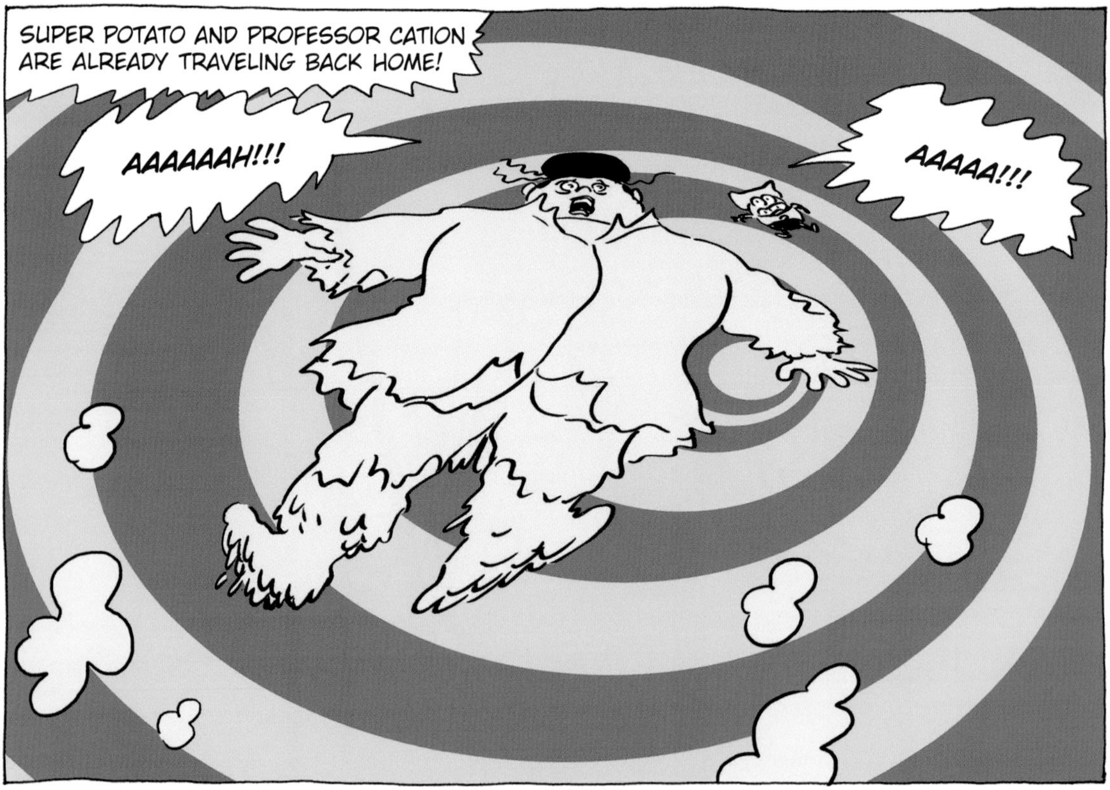
SUPER POTATO AND PROFESSOR CATION ARE ALREADY TRAVELING BACK HOME!
AAAAAAH!!!
AAAAA!!!

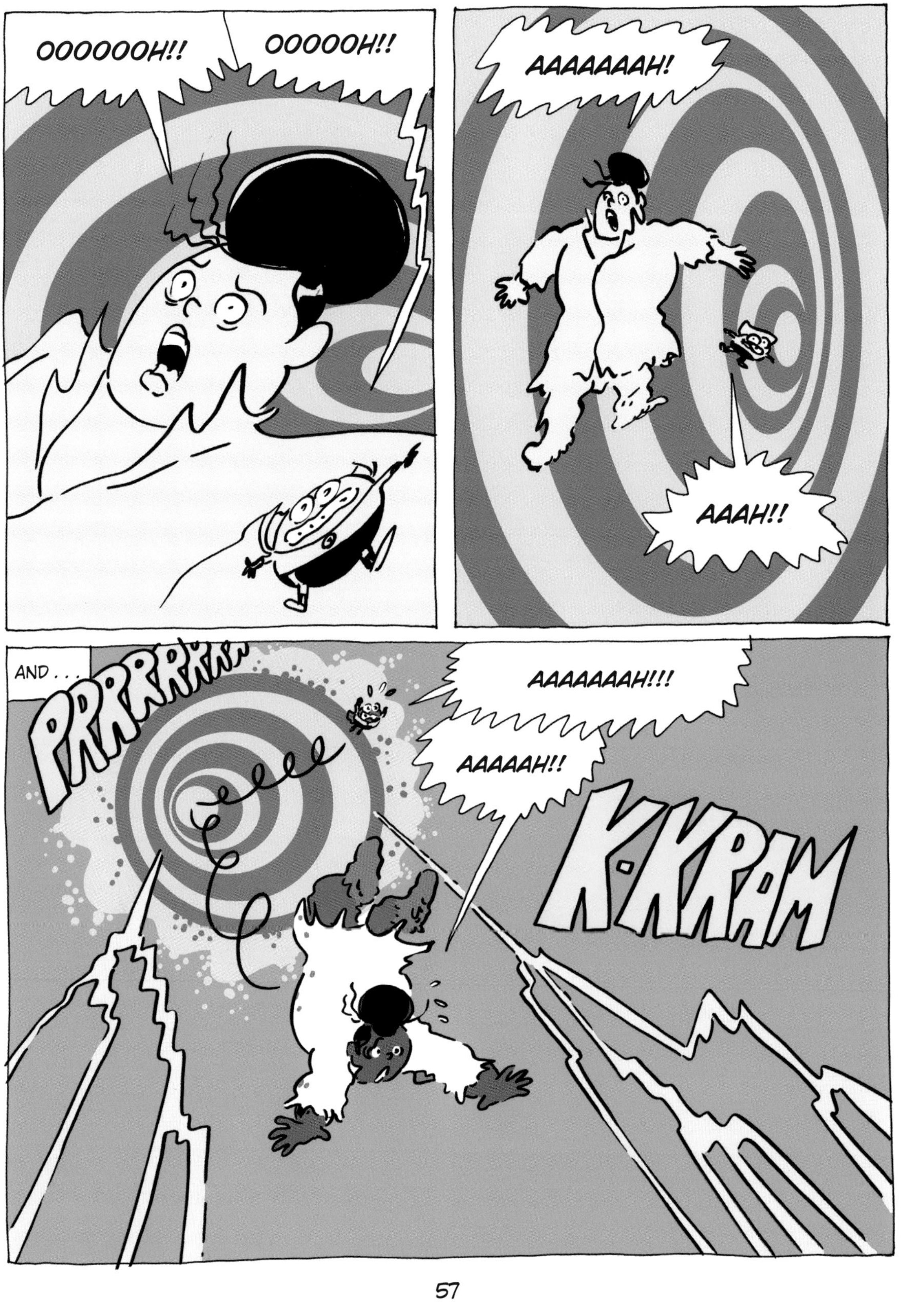
OOOOOOH!!
OOOOOH!!
AAAAAAAH!
AAAH!!
AND . . .
PRRRRRR
AAAAAAAH!!!
AAAAAH!!
K-KRAM

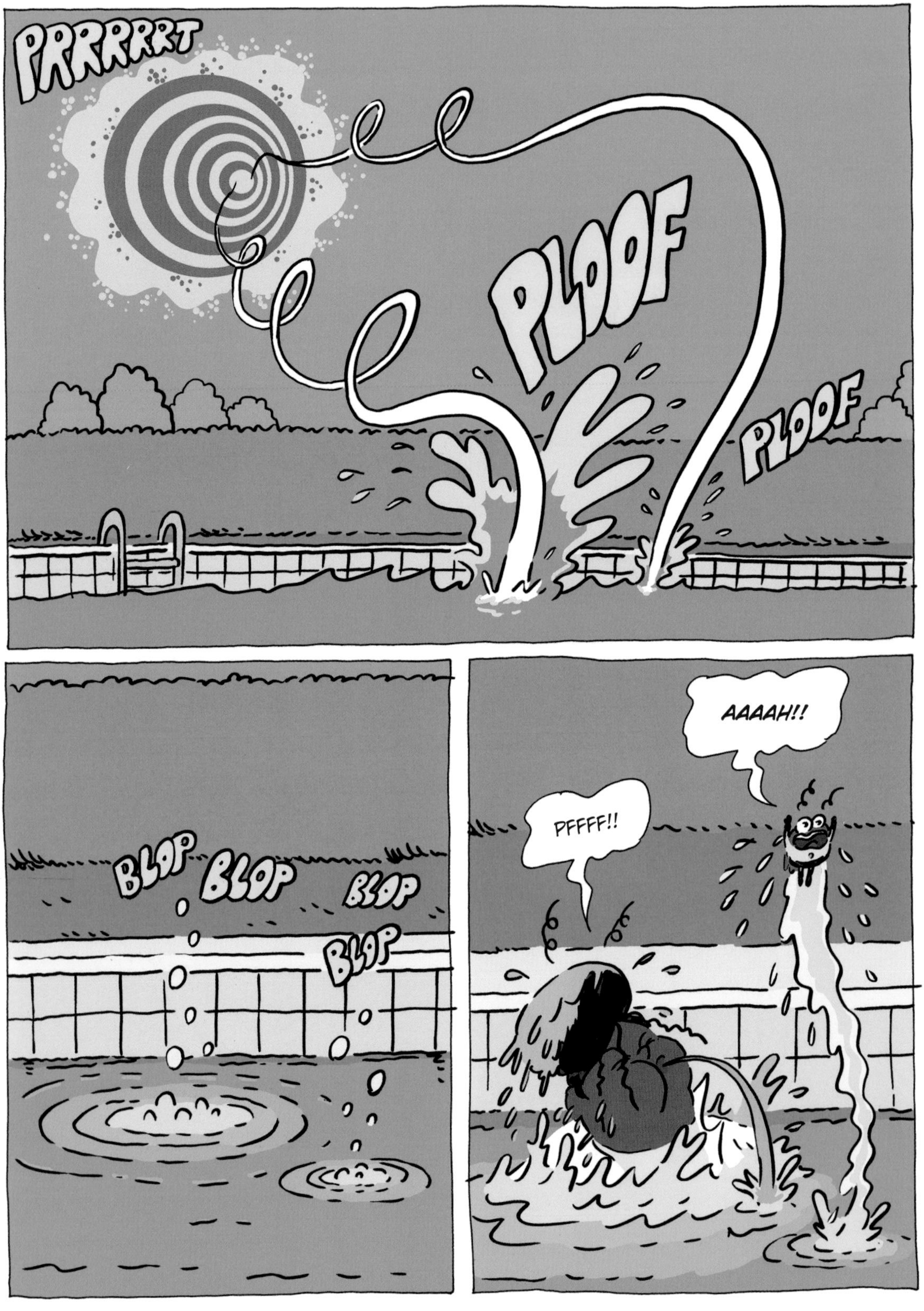
PRRRRRT
PLOOF
PLOOF
BLOP
BLOP
BLOP
BLOP
AAAAH!!
PFFFF!!

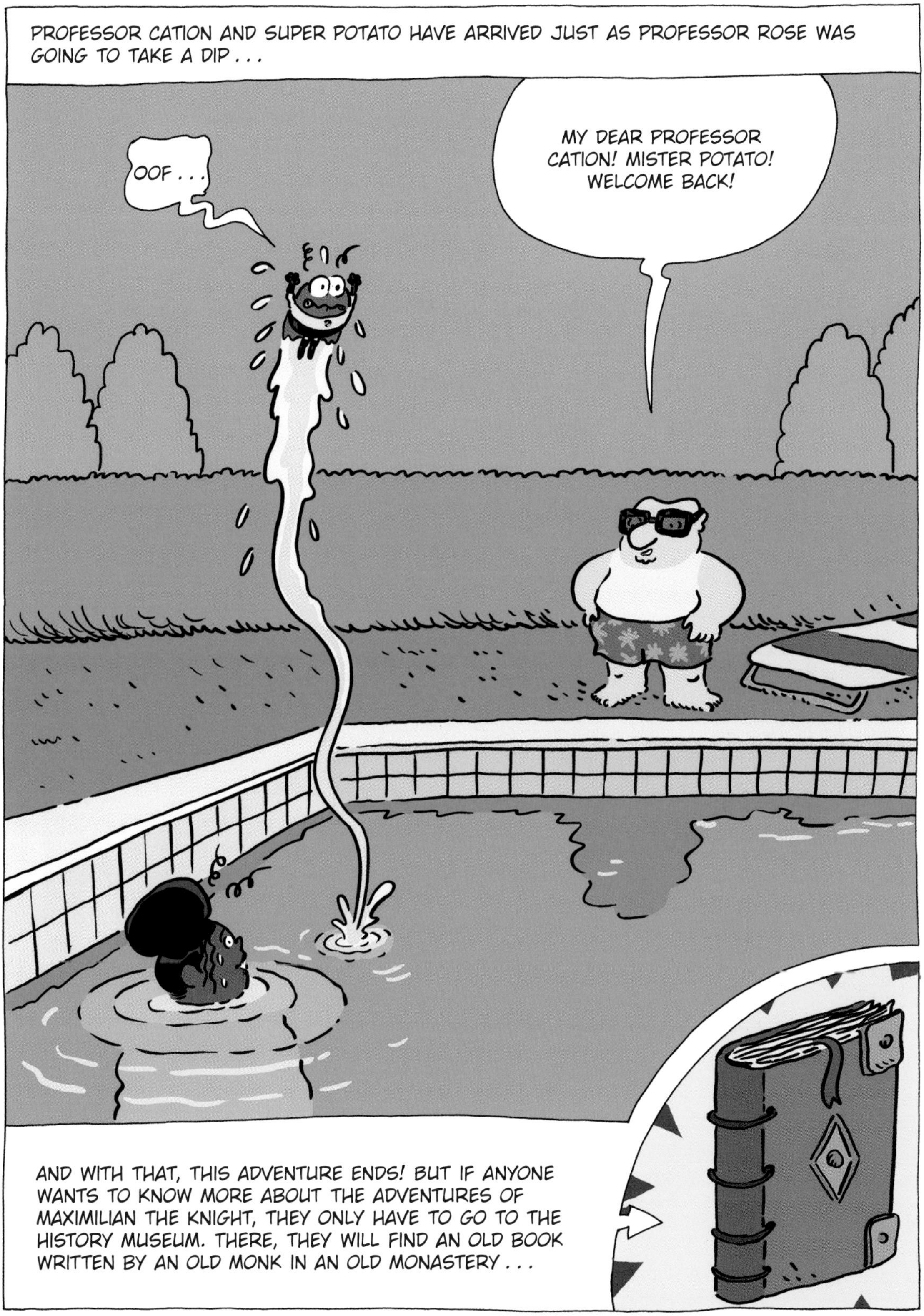
PROFESSOR CATION AND SUPER POTATO HAVE ARRIVED JUST AS PROFESSOR ROSE WAS GOING TO TAKE A DIP . . .
OOF . . .
MY DEAR PROFESSOR CATION! MISTER POTATO! WELCOME BACK!
AND WITH THAT, THIS ADVENTURE ENDS! BUT IF ANYONE WANTS TO KNOW MORE ABOUT THE ADVENTURES OF MAXIMILIAN THE KNIGHT, THEY ONLY HAVE TO GO TO THE HISTORY MUSEUM. THERE, THEY WILL FIND AN OLD BOOK WRITTEN BY AN OLD MONK IN AN OLD MONASTERY . . .

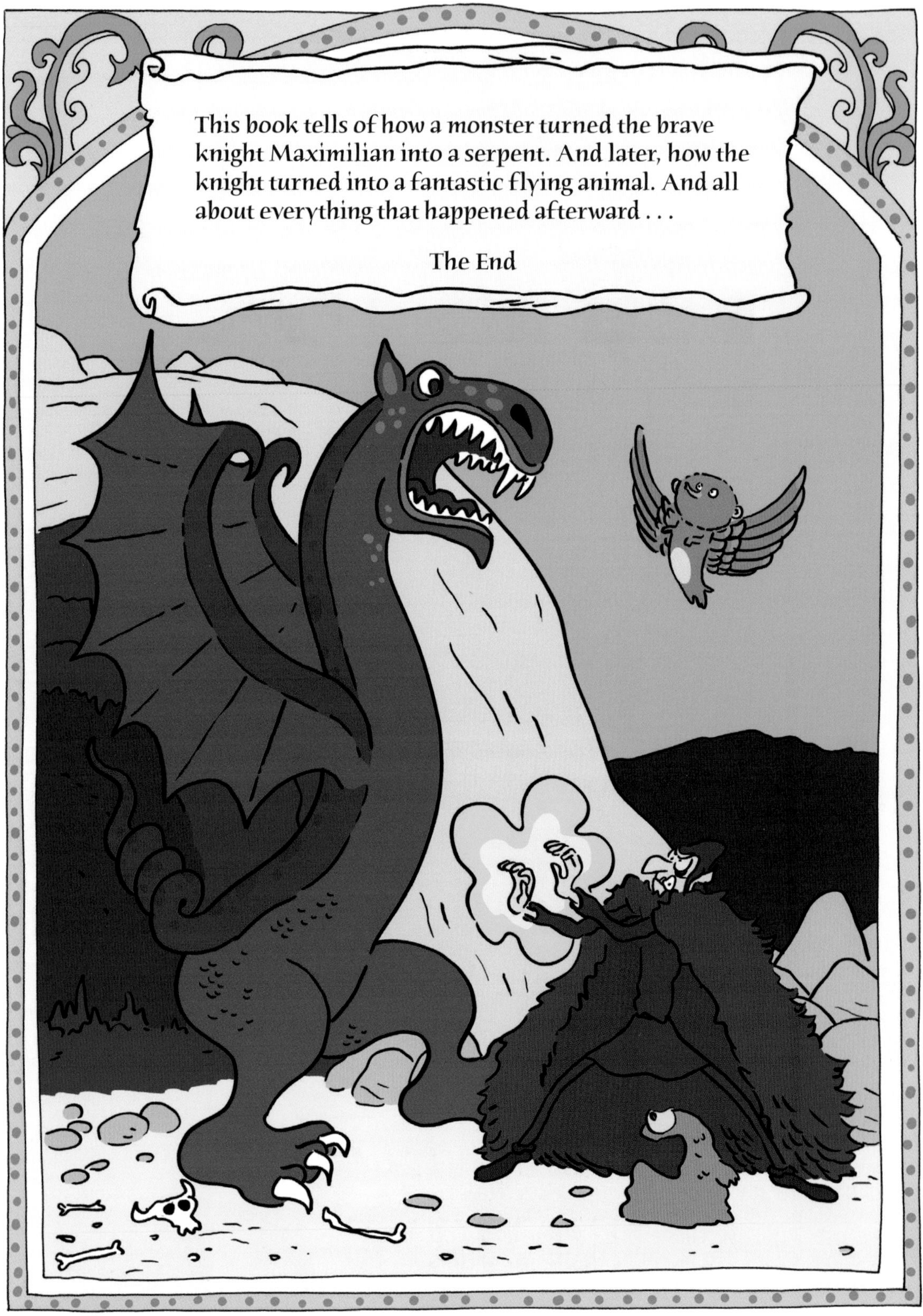
This book tells of how a monster turned the brave knight Maximilian into a serpent. And later, how the knight turned into a fantastic flying animal. And all about everything that happened afterward . . .
The End

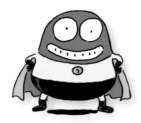

For more hilarious tales of Super Potato, check out . . .

SUPER POTATO
#1 THE EPIC ORIGIN OF SUPER POTATO
Artur Laperla

SUPER POTATO
#2 SUPER POTATO'S GALACTIC BREAKOUT
Artur Laperla

SUPER POTATO
#3 SUPER POTATO'S MEGA TIME-TRAVEL ADVENTURE
Artur Laperla

SUPER POTATO
#4 SUPER POTATO AND THE MUTANT ANIMAL MAYHEM
Artur Laperla

SUPER POTATO
#5 SUPER POTATO AND THE CASTLE OF ROBOTS
Artur Laperla

SUPER POTATO
#6 SUPER POTATO GETS BUFF
Artur Laperla

SUPER POTATO
#7 SUPER POTATO AND THE GREENHOUSE OF EVIL
Artur Laperla

SUPER POTATO
#8 SUPER POTATO AND THE SOARING TERROR OF THE PTEROSAUR
Artur Laperla

SUPER POTATO
#9 SUPER POTATO'S ALL-NIGHT DINOSAUR FIGHT
Artur Laperla

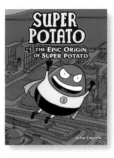

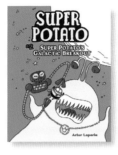

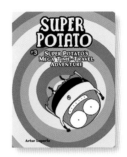

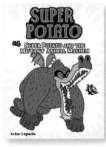

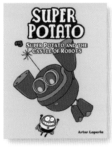

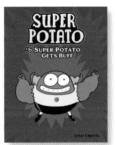

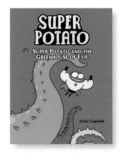

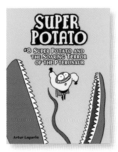

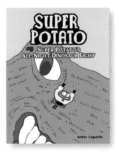

AND TURN THE PAGE FOR A PREVIEW OF OUR HERO'S NEXT ADVENTURE . . .

SUPER POTATO #11

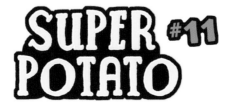

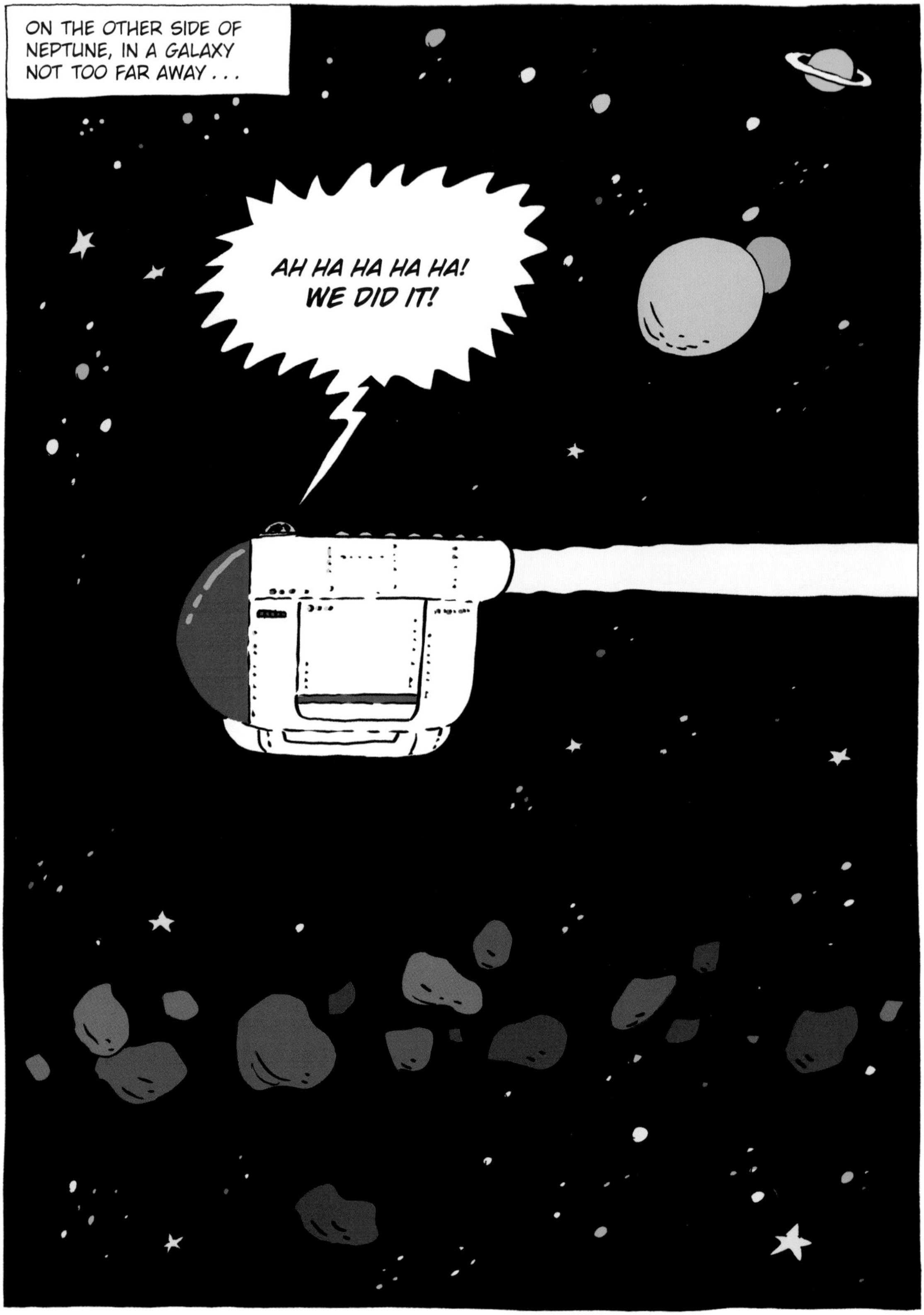
ON THE OTHER SIDE OF NEPTUNE, IN A GALAXY NOT TOO FAR AWAY . . .
AH HA HA HA HA! WE DID IT!

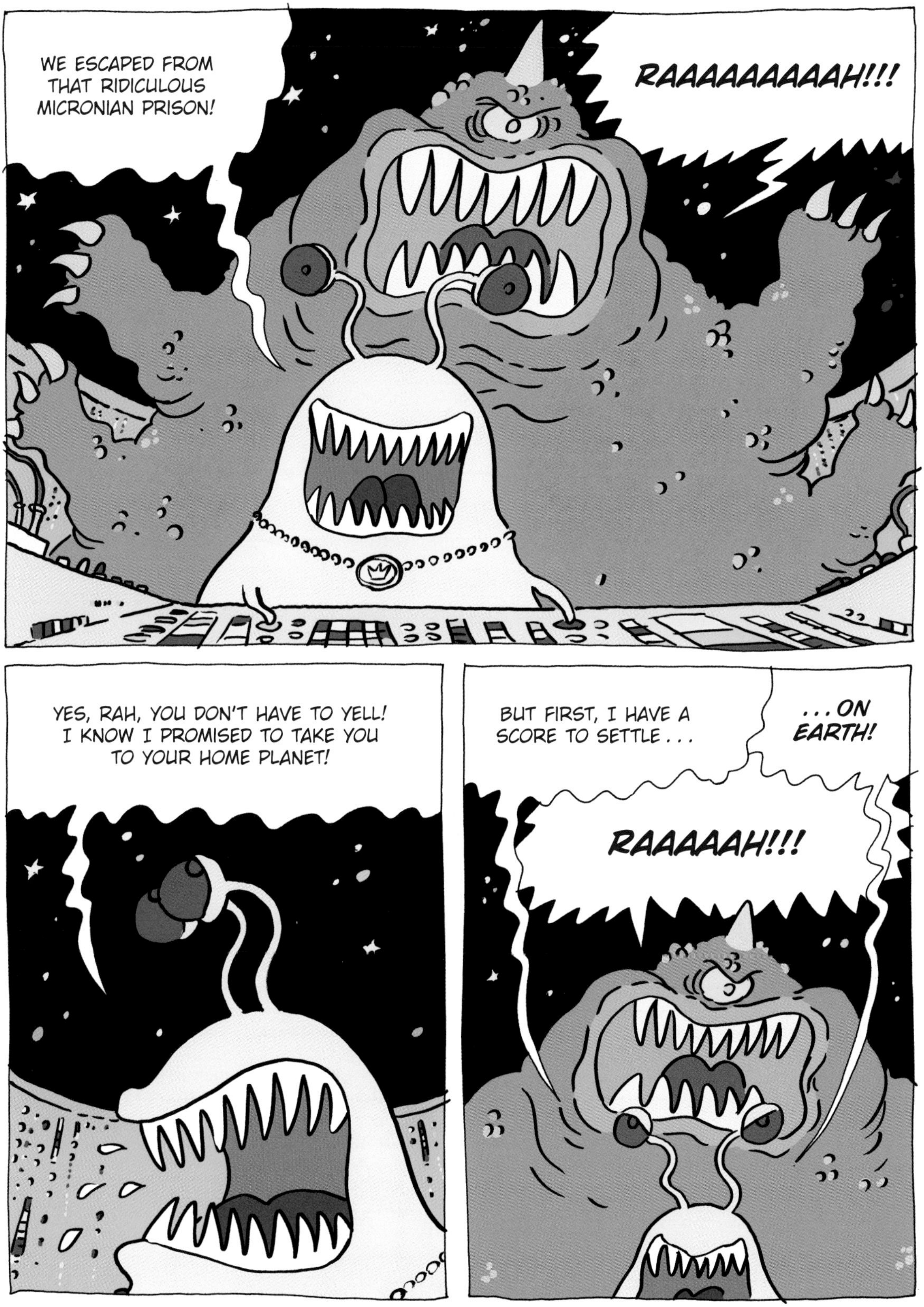
WE ESCAPED FROM THAT RIDICULOUS MICRONIAN PRISON!
RAAAAAAAAAH!!!
YES, RAH, YOU DON'T HAVE TO YELL! I KNOW I PROMISED TO TAKE YOU TO YOUR HOME PLANET!
BUT FIRST, I HAVE A SCORE TO SETTLE . . .
. . . ON EARTH!
RAAAAAH!!!

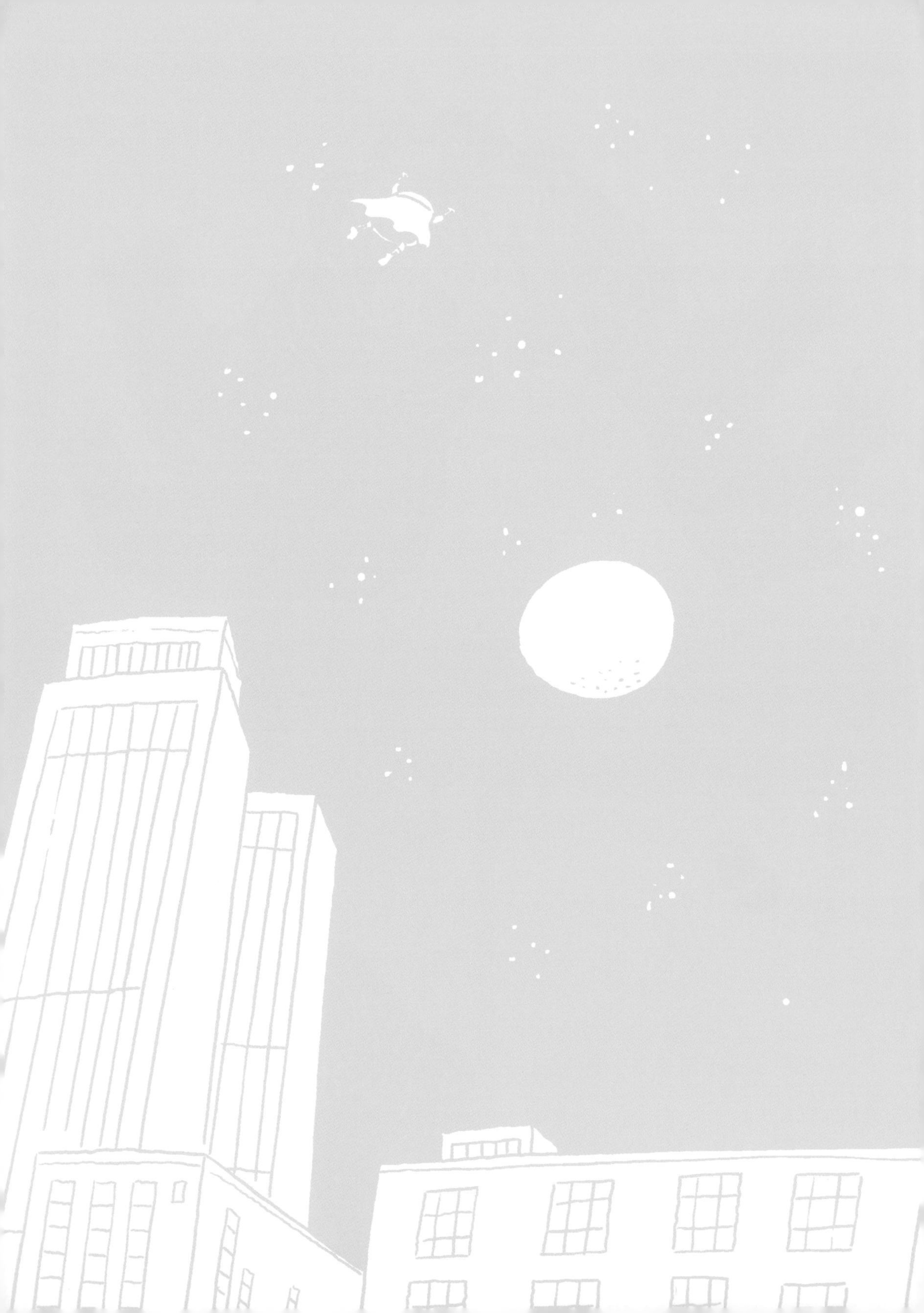